KILL ME GENTLY,
DARLING

**Other Five Star Titles
by Barbara Faith:**

The Sun Dancers

KILL ME GENTLY, DARLING

Barbara Faith

Five Star
Unity, Maine

Five Star Romance Series
Published in 2000 in conjunction with Maureen Moran
Agency.

The text of this edition is unabridged.

Set in 11 pt. Plantin by Anne Bradeen.

Printed in the United States on permanent paper.

Library of Congress Cataloging-in-Publication Data

Faith, Barbara.
    Kill me gently, darling / Barbara Faith.
        p.   cm.
    ISBN 0-7862-2637-4 (hc : alk. paper)
    1. Drug traffic — Fiction. 2. Hurricanes — Fiction.
    3. Jamaica — Fiction.   I. Title.
PS3556.A3659 K55 2000
    813′.54—dc21   00-035360

KILL ME GENTLY,
DARLING

CHAPTER ONE

When the phone rang, Bruce jerked against my hip. I reached for it on the fifth ring and he gave me a look that made me wish I hadn't.

"Hello," I said, ignoring his baleful green eyes.

"Darling, you're still asleep."

I tried to stifle a yawn. "More or less, Mary. More or less. What time is it?"

"Nearly noon. Are you all right?"

"Tired. I fixed coffee earlier and came back to bed with Bruce and the *Times*."

"How is he?"

"Miserable." I shifted my hip against his weight and said, "Move dammit."

He rose slowly, and, step by careful step, marched up my body. He stopped inches from my face and yowled.

I heard a gasp and chuckle from the other end of the phone. "So I woke the monster. Why in the world do you put up with him?"

"Well . . . he was dad's."

"Now, Catherine. Really, dear, you musn't . . ."

"I know."

"I called to ask you to come over this afternoon. I'm having some people in."

"Not today, Mary. It's raining."

7

"Laura and Kitty are coming. And Mark Colby. You remember him. And a couple of men I met the other night. We'll have a nice cozy Sunday. A few drinks by the fire and Lucie will be back in time to scrounge some dinner for us."

"Next time. I promise."

"Catherine, I know how you feel about your father, but it's time you got out. I'm not going to let you mope around that apartment all day Sunday with only that dreadful orange cat for company. Alan—he's one of the men I met the other night—lives somewhere near you. I'll phone and ask him to pick you up."

"But . . ."

"Wait till you see him, Catherine. Too young for me, but what the hell. Be nice to him. But just remember, I've got dibs."

"Mary, honestly, I appreciate what you're trying to do, but I just don't feel like going out."

"I know you don't, dear. But believe me, you'll feel better for it. And besides, I've got a lovely surprise for you."

When I put the phone down I scratched the miserable cat behind the ears and winced while his nails clawed my shoulder ecstatically. Mary was right, he was a dreadful cat. But he was the last link I had left with my father. "He was the only person you ever liked, wasn't he, Bruce!" I said. His answer was a slow blink of mean, green eyes.

When we came back from the hospital the night my father died, Isabel, my step-mother, said, "The first thing I'm going to do is get rid of that goddamned cat."

And I said, "No, I'll take him."

I was damned if I'd let her kill the only thing that had made life in that house bearable for my father the last few years of his life.

As it turned out, Bruce was the only thing I got. I was entitled to half of what the house was worth, but Isabel said, "When I sell it, you'll get your share, Catherine. Until then it's my home."

She sold all the antiques that had come from my mother's side of the family, and all of the books in dad's library.

"To hell with it," I said now. "I've got you, you rotten cat."

Yes, I had Bruce and a case of the blues that was hanging on much longer than it should have. I knew it, but I didn't know what to do about it. All I wanted to do was stay in my apartment and sleep. And try to forget the terrible last three months of my father's illness. I'd had four assignments, one very good one to do the illustrations for a new hotel in Connecticut. But I'd turned them down. I *knew* I should get back to work. I *knew* I should get up and dress every morning. I *knew* Mary was trying to be kind by insisting I stir my bones. And, oh God, I *knew* it was wrong to cling to my grief. But I couldn't seem to help myself.

I washed my hair and made myself do my makeup carefully, wondering as I did about the new man in Mary's life. What was he like? Too young for her, she'd said. I hoped, for her sake, he was nice. Mary needed a change of luck.

I dressed in a wine velour pants suit and a pink blouse, and was ready when the buzzer sounded.

"Alan Carlisle," a voice said. "Mary's friend,"

I pushed the button to release the downstairs door.

He was tall. He was tan. And lean. A combination of all the good-looking young men who have ever posed for bathing trunks, tennis clubs, or resort ads. His slightly tilted eyes were a strange light green. I pegged him Princeton, class of '68.

"Hi," I said, offering my hand. "I'm Catherine. With a C. Is it still raining?"

"How about Cathy? With a C. Yes, it's still raining."

Bruce jumped off the top of the sofa when he saw me reach for my coat and went to stand by the front door.

"No," I said. "You're not going out. I am. You can fend for yourself this afternoon."

"Hey, fella," Alan said.

And before I could say, "No, don't . . ." he bent down to pet Bruce, who gave one of his ungodly yowls, lightninged out a paw, and dug his claws into Alan's hand.

Alan drew back, astonished. "Cats *like* me," he said.

"Not this cat. He doesn't like anybody."

"Not even you?"

"Not particularly. He tolerates me because I feed him. I'm awfully sorry. Come on in the bathroom and I'll clean the scratch."

His hand was strong, smooth, and very clean.

"Iodine or alcohol?" I asked.

"Iodine. Why in the world do you keep him?"

"He belonged to my dad. When dad died two months ago, my step-mother wanted to put Bruce to sleep. I couldn't let her do it. Dad loved him and . . ."

"Of course you couldn't. Maybe he'll mellow in time."

"He's ten years old. I'm afraid it's now or never."

We smiled at each other.

"You look like a strawberry soda," he said.

I gave his hand back to him.

"How old were you when you acquired a step-mother?" he asked.

"Fourteen."

"A lonely age."

"Made bearable by Mary and her younger sister, Liz. I spent most of my time with them. Mary was awfully good to me. She got me my first magazine job when I came to New York."

"You're a writer?"

"No, Mary's the writer. I'm an illustrator. I do the illustrations for her children's books." I looked up at him. "How long have you known her?"

"A week or so. We met at a party. She's . . . uh . . . quite a lively gal." His voice was careful.

"Oh?" Now my voice was careful.

"She got pretty high on coke."

I stared at him. "She may have had a bit too much to drink," I said coldly. "She sometimes does. But she doesn't bother with anything else. I'm sure you're mistaken."

"Perhaps."

I turned away from him. I decided I didn't like him and I hoped Mary was not completely gone on him.

She was. She latched onto him the minute we arrived at her apartment, while I went to say hello to Laura Jennings and Kitty Delaney. Laura, an attractive woman in her early sixties, is an especially good friend. We see a good bit of each other whenever she's in town. But she's an avid golfer and is forever off somewhere to follow the sun and chase that small white ball around a golf course.

Kitty is plump and pretty and oddly girlish. She's a huggable woman with a froth of gray curls atop her head. And, as long as I've known her, she's always had a man around to hug her.

Mark is . . . well, Mark is Mark. Twenty-five or so. In love with the theatre and three or four chorus boys. Every time he gets a job the show folds. He's incredibly sweet and the only person I've ever known who actually takes chicken soup to sick friends. Now I offered my cheek for his perfunctuory kiss, accepted the drink he gave me, and moved to the fireplace.

"All set, darling?" Mary asked. "Come warm your bones. And say hello to Whitey Koebler. Whitey this is my oldest and dearest friend, Catherine Adams."

My first impression of Whitey Koebler, my lasting impression, was of total whiteness. Not Caucasian white, but pasty, deadly white—his face, his hair, his eyelashes and brows, his white spatula fingers that curled around the glass. Even his eyes were such a light, cold gray that they too seemed white.

I moved closer to the fire.

"Hiya," he said.

"How do you do?"

"So you're a pal of Mary's."

"Yes."

"She's quite a broad."

My smile was stiff. Good Lord, where had Mary found him?

It was a long afternoon. We had several more drinks and a light dinner when Mary's maid, Lucie, arrived. I wondered when I could decently leave, I longed for the quiet of my own apartment, for the strange comfort of my antisocial cat.

I chatted with Laura and Kitty, and tried to avoid Whitey. But his stone gray eyes followed me around the room, moving from my face to my breasts, speculative and cold.

"Isn't he weird?" Laura whispered. "I don't like the way he looks at you."

"Neither do I. Where in the world do you suppose Mary found him?"

"I think she met both of them, Alan and Whitey, at a party at Midge Cooper's. Alan's all right, but this . . . !"

"They're friends, I think."

"Alan doesn't seem to have too much to say to him. But of course Mary's not giving Alan a chance to talk to anybody."

I looked over at Mary, small and dark and alive, her arm

hooked through Alan's, laughing up into his face. I remembered what he'd said about her earlier this afternoon. I was sure it wasn't true, but it worried me. Mary had been on edge, restless, since her last divorce. She laughed too loud and played too hard. But drugs? I didn't think so. I doubted that she'd ever done anything more than smoke a little grass.

At eight-thirty I told Mary I was going home.

"But it's early," she said. "You'll do no such thing."

"I'm tired, Mary. And I've got to get an early start in the morning."

"A job?" Her bright black eyes looked inquiring. She knew I hadn't worked since dad's death.

"I've decided to take the Connecticut job."

"Don't."

"Don't? But you're the one who's been telling me to get back to work."

"But I've got a job for you myself. I'm doing a book about Jamaica and I want you to do the illustrations."

"I don't know anything about Jamaica, Mary."

"What's to know, darling? Sun and rum. I'll give you the manuscript tonight and, if you like the book, then go to Jamaica. You'll need to get island backgrounds. I want you to sketch the Blue Mountains, Fern Gully, Dunns River Falls. Everything. Jamaica's like no other place in the world. You have to see it for yourself to know what I mean. You have to see the incredible turquoise color of the Caribbean with your own eyes." She put her arm around my shoulders. "I want you to go, darling. I want you to swim and sun and start to work again. It's time you pulled yourself out of the doldrums."

"I know, Mary, but . . ."

"Jamaica's lovely in April, Catherine. I've got a house on the beach. Compliments of James Alexander Montgomery, II.

Was he my third or my fourth husband? Anyway, he built this perfectly lovely house for me. I've got a woman by the name of Euphemia who takes care of it. You'll have a marvelous, relaxing time. Maybe I'll join you in a week or two."

"I'll think about it," I said doubtfully. And then I said it was late, I had a headache, and I really had to go. She got a copy of the manuscript, tucked it under my arm, and said, "Only if you promise you'll read this tonight."

I kissed her, said goodnight to Kitty and Laura, accepted Mark Colby's second perfunctory kiss of the evening, and turned to say goodbye to Whitey and to Alan.

Whitey was not a tall man. We stood almost eye to eye. He put his hand out. I took it and felt the pressure of his fingers against mine. He leaned forward, and the cold lips touched my cheek as Mark's had done.

"I'll take you home," he said.

"No, I . . ." I couldn't think. I felt panic rise in my throat.

"Sorry, pal," Alan said. "I always take home the gal what I brung."

"That's not necessary," I said. My glance swung from Alan to Whitey and back to Alan again. "But I'd appreciate it if you'd see me to a cab."

When the cab came, he opened the door to help me in and said, "I'd like to see you again, Cathy."

"I'm going to be pretty busy." I held Mary's script up. "And I may go to Jamaica."

"Maybe we could have dinner before you leave—if you do decide to go."

"Maybe." I kept my voice noncommittal.

On the way to my apartment I thought, 'I still don't like you, Alan. And even if I did, Mary's got a very special light in her eyes when she looks at you.'

Bruce was moderately glad to see me. I opened a can of cat

food, which he sniffed disdainfully before he settled down to eat. I undressed, made myself a Swiss cheese sandwich, and went to bed with Mary's manuscript. I had no intention of going to Jamaica, but it wouldn't hurt to read the book. Bruce wandered in and settled himself against my hip as I began to read. *Island boy*, by Mary Bernardi.

I liked it. It was funny and charming and touching. But when I finished it and turned the light off, I was still determined not to go to Jamaica.

When the phone rang I switched on the light and squinted at the clock. It was three o'clock. "Hello," I said.

"I want to screw you," the voice said.

"What?"

"I want to screw you until you yell. I want to bite those cute little knockers of yours, and . . ."

I slammed the phone down. My hands were shaking. I had recognized the voice. The white voice.

I reached down and pulled Bruce up to my chest, hugging him against me, ignoring his yowls of protests.

The phone rang again at seven.

"I'll hurt you so good," he said, "all up and down the whole golden length of you. And when I'm screwing you I'll . . ."

"Stop it!" I shouted. "Stop it, you bastard."

And at noon.

"You might even like it, Catsy-baby. When I get through with you . . ."

I was crying when I slarnmed the phone down.

And when I stopped crying I phoned Mary and told her that yes, I would do the illustrations for her book. I would go to Jamaica.

CHAPTER TWO

It was an island in the sun, just as Mary had promised. As the plane made the final approach to the airport in Montego Bay, I could see the white-foam wave-tops breaking against the reefs. The water was blue there, a deep endless blue, but inshore it became turquoise. And it seemed to me on the two-hour ride to Ocho Rios that I'd never been so aware of color—the rose-pink, red, and purple bougainvillaea that covered the seaside houses, the scarlet flowered tulip trees, and the tall, slender palms that leaned into the trade winds.

A week had passed since the party at Mary's. She was surprised, too, at my sudden burst of energy. I hurried through the packing, the reservation, the carrier for Bruce, the closing of the apartment in a fever of anxiety. And although I'd had my phone number changed, I jumped every time it rang.

Now as we drove along the narrow highway I could feel the tension of the last week slipping away.

"We're almost there, Bruce," I said. "I'll let you out as soon as we arrive and you can run to your heart's content."

Mary's house sat on a small rise just fifty yards from the beach. Palms, feathery green bamboo, and hibiscus fringed three sides. Green, mist-covered mountains huddled in the background.

Euphemia was a large woman with a smooth, unlined face and calm brown eyes. She wore an old-fashioned Mother

Hubbard dress. Her hair was covered by a blue flowered kerchief. She showed me the house; four bedrooms, a living
room, a diningroom, a large kitchen, a den. And a terrace that
ran the whole length of the house and faced the sea. James Alexander Montgomery II had indeed done very well by Mary.

Over breakfast the next morning I told Euphemia that I
needed a boy to pose for me.

She chuckled. "I got eleven boys," she said. "Tomorrow I
bring them and you choose."

I looked at them the next morning. They looked at me.
The one on the very end was as cute as a button, but he was
too young, not more than two and a half. My eyes traveled up
the line of feet-shuffling, giggling boys. The one in the middle
grinned and I made my decision. Seven years old. Skinny and
long-legged as a crane. With skin the color of taffy, and big
black eyes that were fringed with long, dark lashes.

"The middle boy," I said to Euphemia. "If it's all right
with you."

"Surely it be all right, Mistress." She beckoned to the boy.
"Come over here, Samuel, and say how-do to Mistress
Catherine."

The other boys, looking somewhat relieved, I thought,
started back down to the beach. All except the little one.

"You go on with your brothers, Moses," Euphemia said.

I felt Bruce brush past my legs.

"Go now," Euphemia repeated.

"Won't," Moses said. He came and stood over Bruce.

"Don't touch the cat," I said. "He's kinda mean."

Moses gave me a dirty look, and before I could stop him he
bent down and scooped Bruce up in his arms.

"He'll scratch you," I said anxiously.

"Won't," he said.

Boy and cat regarded me with cool 'don't-bother-us-lady'

17

looks. Bruce seemed quite contented as Moses carried him off down toward the beach.

"Euphemia . . ." I started.

"Now don't you fret, Mistress Catherine. Moses won't hurt the cat."

"It's not the cat I'm worried about," I said.

When I explained to Samuel that the work I wanted him to do consisted of playing in the waves, on the shore, and just plain fooling around, he shook his head in amazement. And when a delighted grin split his boy face and crinkled his eyes, I knew he was the perfect child for Mary's book.

Euphemia and I had agreed on a reasonable salary for Samuel—one dollar a week for him—the rest would be banked by his mama.

We'd been working together for a week when one morning he poked me on the shoulder and whispered, "That man be watching us."

"Let's just pretend he's not there and maybe he'll go away," I whispered back.

"I don't think so, Mistress. I think he be going to come here."

The man, who had been watching us from the shade of a palm tree, got up and ambled over. He was tall and broad and he walked like a policeman. He smiled down at Samuel and ruffled the boy's hair with a big hand. And to me he said, "You're going to dry up like a prune if you don't get out of the sun. Are you an artist?"

"Illustrator."

"What are you illustrating?"

I sighed. He obviously wasn't going to be easy to get rid of. "A children's book."

"What's it about?"

"A little boy who lives in Jamaica with his mother, his

grandmother, his three maiden aunts, and his fourteen sisters."

"Kee-rist!

I frowned.

"What do you think about that, boy?" he asked.

Samuel shrugged. "I tell her I got no sisters. I got ten brothers but no sisters."

The man grinned. A nice grin. "You must have quite a mama."

"I do, man. She be Euphemia. Everybody knows Euphemia."

"I bet they do." He swallowed a smile. "Well, I know you're Samuel, and I know your mother is Euphemia. What about the artist lady?"

"That be Mistress Adams."

"And does Mistress Adams have a first name?"

"Catherine-with-a-C," I said.

"How do you do. I'm David-with-a-D."

He squatted down on the sand and I looked at him. His nose was crooked and his forehead was lined. His salt and pepper hair was pleasantly shaggy. His eyes were the color of cinnamon. He took the straw hat off my head and fanned himself. "Are you staying at the hotel?"

"No, I've got a house on the beach."

"And you write children's books."

"No. I only illustrate them. Mary Bernardi writes them. It's her house I'm staying in."

"And what about you, fella?" He turned to Samuel. "Why aren't you in school?"

"Sometimes I be. Sometimes I not be. Sometimes work loading the bananas."

"Hey! Well, listen, I'd like to see that. How about taking me with you next time a banana boat comes in?"

19

"You want to see the banana boats? Sure, I take you. There be boats from all over the world. You want a job?"

"No. I've already got a job."

"What do you do?"

David hesitated for the briefest fraction of a second. Then he said, "This and that. Mostly I'm a travel writer."

"A travel writer? That's not what you look like," I said.

"Oh? And what *do* I look like?"

"A cop. You *walk* like a cop."

"And are you an authority on cops?"

"I'm not an authority on anything. I'm an artist. I suppose I study people—their characteristics—without meaning to. You look like a policeman."

"Don't try to pidgeonhole me, Mistress Catherine." His voice had an edge to it. "I'm a travel writer. I'm doing a book on the Caribbean. That's why I'm in Jamaica."

"O.K.," I said, feeling as though my feathers had been ruffled.

After Samuel left, David and I settled in the shade under the palm trees. He picked up my sketch pad and thumbed through it, smiling occasionally. "This is good. You like kids?"

"Sure. Doesn't everybody?"

"Have any of your own?"

"Nope. I'm not married." And then I dug a hole in the sand with my toes while I tried to think of a way to ask him if he were married. Which was pretty silly, because it couldn't matter in the slightest to me. In the first place, he was too old for me. Forty-two at least. In the second place, he was just a strange man on a strange beach. When we finished our conversation he'd walk up the beach and I'd walk down the beach. Still . . . "What about you? Children?"

"A boy. One boy. His name is Davey."

A strange sinking feeling while I thought, unreasonably, damn, he *is* married. But when I asked how old his son was, my voice was pleasantly interested.

"He's twenty-two now. He was eighteen when he went away."

"Went away?"

"Vietnam." His fist doubled. His knuckles dug hard into the sand, where they found a seashell. They twisted, turned and ground against the sharpness. "He's been listed as Missing in Action for four years."

As gently as I could I lifted his hand away from the cutting edge of the shell. "I'm sorry," I said.

"It's been a long time. A purgatory of a time. I'm sure he's alive, but it's hell not knowing where he is. Imagining him locked up in some stinking hole. I've got friends in the State Department working on it. And there's someone else—a man who knows a few people in the Middle East. He's working on it too. I'll get Davey back. I know that some day I'll get him back."

He looked out at the sea. "It was hard on Elinor, my wife. Rather, my ex-wife. She divorced me before Davey went to 'Nam. We tried to get back together later, but there wasn't anything left. We hadn't been able to make it with him, and we couldn't make it without him. Jesus! Let's talk about something else."

We talked about a lot of things that afternoon. In between the talking there were long minutes of just looking at the sky, watching the gulls float white-winged above us. Once we ran down to the beach. The sun burned our feet, and so we ran until we fell into the water, then laughed with pleasure at the cool salt sting of it against our skin. We laughed until a wave bounced us together then we stopped laughing and moved apart.

When we came out of the water he said, "Will you have dinner with me tonight?"

"Hmmm," I said, pretending to think it over.

When I got back to the beach house I went into the bathroom and looked at myself in the mirror. And groaned. Two weeks at Arden's wouldn't even dent the surface. I stripped out of the suit, frowned at my salt wet hair, and got under the shower. The hot water stung my sunburn, but I scrubbed myself down and washed my hair. When I got out, I had one terrible moment of sheer panic that I wouldn't be able to find Mary's electric rollers. But I did.

The white pants suit had a high neck and a low back that did nice things for my sunburn-cumtan. In fact, the back of me looked a lot better than the front of me. I'm not exactly a raving beauty. I envy women with 42-inch busts, high cheekbones, and Grecian noses. My nose is just a nose and my mouth is bigger than I would have chosen. When I was twelve I saw an ad that guaranteed a process that would make dimples for the low, low price of fifty cents a dimple. *Voila!* The dimples would surely give me an instant beauty. But my letter was returned marked "out of business." At fourteen I saw another ad that promised a magic lotion that would enlarge my pea-size breasts. The lotion gave me pimples. And so I've had to make do with an every-day kind of face and a thirty-four inch bust.

There were some red flowers in the vase on the dresser. I took one, held it to the low V in the back of my pantsuit, and peered at my reflection in the mirror. If I walked backwards all evening I'd be a smash.

Suddenly I felt alive again. All the sadness and the grief, even the tension of the ugliness of Whitey Koebler's phone calls, seemed far away. When the chimes rang I ran all the way to the front door.

Do you know how great, how really great, a big ugly man can look when he's all cleaned up and wearing a dinner jacket? That's the way David looked.

We grinned at each other for about ninety seconds. I handed him the red flower and asked him to pin the posie on the lady. He played it straight, pinned the blossom carefully in place, turned me around, and said, "You're a hell of a good-looking woman, Catherine."

And *that's* what a woman needs to make her feel beautiful.

We had several Planter's Punches. And little bean-size oysters and broiled crawfish. He showed his age when we danced, because he held me close. And, oh my goodness, I liked the man feel of the way his shoulder moved against my fingers. We didn't talk or hum into each other's ear. We didn't have to. We were communicating.

We danced until the orchestra folded and then we sat over a last drink until the candle on the table burned low. Somebody strummed a guitar and sang in a soft Jamaican voice:

> "Oh island in the sun
> Willed to me by my father's hand,
> All my days I will sing in praise
> Of your shining waters, your burning sand."

When we went back down the beach, I took my shoes off so I could feel the sand, soft and yielding beneath my feet. The night was clear. The moon was fat and full and yellow and it made a shimmering golden path on the water.

I handed him the key when we got to the house. When he opened the door I stuck my hand out, suddenly shy, and said, "Goodnight, David. It's been lovely." My voice was hearty.

He smiled at me, leaned forward, and kissed my nose. "Meet you on the beach tomorrow," he said. And then he was gone.

I closed the door and leaned my back against it. "What did you expect" I said aloud.

I toed out of my shoes and walked away from the door. As I did, I heard him hallooing. The halloo got closer and then he was pounding on the door. I broke two fingernails getting the bolt unbolted.

He stopped hallooing when I opened the door. He looked at me, his lower lip caught between his teeth. He took a deep breath and said, "I forgot to unpin you."

"Unpin me?"

"The red flower."

"Oh."

"Turn around."

I turned and felt his hands fumbling with the flower. Suddenly there didn't seem to be enough oxygen in the room. His arms went around my waist. I leaned back against him.

"Don't say anything," he said.

I didn't.

"I'll see you for breakfast." He let me go and handed me the wilted red flower.

CHAPTER THREE

"I'm having company for breakfast," I told Euphemia the next morning.

"A man?"

"Yes."

She smiled. "I fix you up nice on the terrace. You sit in the sun all you can. You be too white."

I stood on the terrace and waited for him. At 8:25 he came lumbering up the beach with his policeman's walk. He wore swimming trunks and a shirt and sunglasses, and he carried a brown paper bag in his hand.

He handed it to me. "Present for you," he said.

"A present?" I opened the bag. "Champagne," I said. "Oh, David, champagne for breakfast."

"Only because it's a holiday."

I wrinkled my brow. "You sure?"

"I'm sure. Well, what the hell . . ." He looked embarrassed. "It's our first day."

Just then Euphemia came out on the terrace.

Papaya and mango. Ham and eggs. Champagne. And the smell of the sea. Even Bruce seemed happier than usual as he munched a scrap of David's ham.

After breakfast we went to meet Samuel. He and David swam together while I sketched. I'd meant to do just Samuel, but I found myself sketching the two of them. They

C-1

were such a contrast: the big, shaggy-haired man and the small, brown boy. When they discovered a sea animal, they squatted down, peering at it and, for a moment, their faces had the same child-like look of curiosity and wonder. I sketched as rapidly as I could, knowing somehow that I wanted to keep a record of their man and boy faces.

A little after noon David said he had some work to do and we agreed to meet for dinner. I finished the sketch I was working on and invited Samuel to have lunch with me.

He bobbed his head, looking both eager and shy.

"Hamburgers and fried banana chips?" I asked.

He gave a little-boy whoop and raced up the beach toward the house.

When I caught up to him I said, "You're all hot and perspirey. Better cool off before your Mama sees you or she'll think I've been working you too hard."

"Yes ma'am, Mistress," he agreed. And before I could say anything else he made a flying leap into the water. And just as suddenly made a flying leap *out* of the water. I thought he was playing, and I grinned at him and started up toward the house when I heard his cry of utter and unmistakable anguish. Hopping on one foot, he managed to get to the edge of the water before he collapsed.

When I reached him I saw that his face was twisted in pain and that he was sobbing. Two jet black, incredibly ugly, round sea animals, with spines like black needles, were stuck to his foot.

His sobs became screams as I bent over him. Up at the top of the dune I could see Euphemia scrambling down the sand toward us.

"Pull them out, pull them out," Samuel cried.

I grasped them, one in each hand and felt a suddenly sickening shock of pain.

"Don't be touching them," Euphemia shouted from somewhere behind me.

I bit my lips and pulled. They came out of Samuel's foot, into my hands, the black needle-like spines imbedding deep in my fingers.

Euphemia rushed to Samuel and picked him up in her arms. When she saw my hands she said, "Oh Lord, Lord. You shouldn't have done that. They be sea urchins. You got to use pinchers to get those things out."

"But he was in such pain."

She soothed the still sobbing Samuel, picked him up, and put him over her shoulder. Then she grasped my arm and helped me up the slanting dune.

"I got to get them out of you," she said when we reached the house.

"Take care of Samuel first. Make sure he's O.K. Make sure none of the spines broke off in his foot."

I held my hands in front of me and tried not to look at the black ugliness. I wasn't being heroic. I was trying to put off as long as possible the painful prodding and pulling I knew would have to be done before I got the awful things off of me. And it *was* painful. Euphemia got a pair of pliers from the kitchen. She sat me down at the kitchen table and pulled, first one, then the other from my already swollen hands. Then she got a needle and tweezers and prodded out the spines that had broken off under the skin.

I was wet and shaking by the time she finished. And so was she.

"I think I'll lie down," I said after she'd bathed my hands and covered them with ointment and gauze. Then I remembered David.

"I was going to have dinner with David—Mr. McKenna. Would you phone him for me and tell him that

I won't be able to make it?"

"What about I fix two nice plates and you and the gentleman eat here? Rest a while, and when you wake up you going to feel better. I call him and tell him. I bet he be real glad to have dinner here with you."

She wouldn't leave until he came. And when she was ready she said to him, "You take care of Mistress Catherine. If you want me to come back, you call over to the hotel and tell them to send a boy to get me."

When he promised that he would, she picked Samuel up in her arms and made ready to leave. Before she did, she bobbed her head in a formal little bow and said, "I thank you for what you did for my boy, Mistress."

"Isn't she nice?" I said to David after she'd gone.

He nodded. "Yes, she is. Very nice. I think you've made a friend for life. Do your hands hurt, Catherine?"

"Not as much as they did. The salve Euphemia put on them took most of the pain away. I just hope I can manage a knife and fork."

I couldn't quite. Or perhaps I could have, but it was rather nice, having him sit close to me and help me with each bite I took. After we'd eaten and he'd cleaned the dishes we sat on the terrace and watched the darkness come.

"How long will you be here?" I asked.

"Not too long. Jamaica isn't forever."

He moved to change records. We didn't talk, we just listened to the music and watched the fat red sun settle into the sea. The pain in my hands eased, and I dozed a bit. When he sat down beside me on the chaise I opened my eyes and smiled up at him.

"I'd better shove off and let you get some sleep."

"In a minute."

He touched my bandaged hands very gently. "You're defenseless, Mistress Catherine. I could have my way with you and you'd never be able to fight me off with these. I'd kiss you once and all hell would break loose."

"Naw," I said. "What's in a kiss? A nice friendly way to say goodnight. People do it all the time. It's just a . . ."

"Shut up," he said.

He was right. All hell broke loose.

We slept together that night. No, not slept. Why do people say that, I wonder? Why don't they say, "We loved together that night?" That's what we did, David and I, we loved together. And talked and loved again and were silent, pleasurably silent, listening to night sounds and the soft rush of the waves against the shore. And finally, our hands clasped, we slept.

Bruce came into the room sometime in the night, padding softly in through the French doors. Giving a 'rowrr' of surprise at the stranger in my bed, he stalking heavily over first David's stomach and then mine, to settle finally in his place at my hip.

The gentle awareness that it is morning. The first stirrings, the half sleep. Warmth and skin textures. Small touchings and murmurs. Tentative pressure of leg against leg. Face against his shoulder. Lips against shoulder. Fingertips against breast.

And suddenly the abrupt and awful sound of dishes rattling in the sink.

"Oh, God." I said. "Euphemia."

"Whatzzat?" He raised himself on his elbow. "What's the matter?"

"Euphemia." I nibbled my bottom lip. "She's here. What'll I tell her?"

His fingers worried his shaggy hair. "Tell her you won me in the raffle."

"David!"

"You won't have to tell her anything, Catherine. You're a big girl now."

"I know, I know. And I'm a sexually liberated woman, et cetera, et cetera. But still . . ."

He smiled. "O.K. I'll slip out the French doors. How are your hands?"

I tried to bend my fingers. "Stiff. Help me get the gauze off."

"The swelling has gone down. Maybe hot water will help. Can I help you?"

"No, I'll manage."

"Then I'd better leave."

I bent down and kissed his once or twice broken nose. "No, don't go. We'll try the raffle story on her. Maybe she'll go for it."

He made a grab for me, but I scooted into the bathroom and closed the door.

When I came back, he was standing by the window, looking out at the sea. His back to me. There is something peculiarly touching about a man's bare bottom, and I thought suddenly of how he might have looked as a boy, and I was frightened because he was not young. I had missed his young years. I could never have them. I didn't even know if I could have the years that were left.

"Breakfast in twenty minutes," I said. My breath felt ragged. "The razor's on the sink. It's too small and it's pink and the deodorant's there too and I put some towels out and I found a guest toothbrush . . ."

He turned to look at me, I could see the small pouches under his eyes and the lines around his mouth. And it was then that I began to love him.

I think he knew, because he came to me. He put his hand on the side of my face and rubbed his thumb across my lips. "All right, Catherine," he said. "All right."

CHAPTER FOUR

Once I asked him when he did his work. "When do I give you a chance to work?" I said.

"Mornings. When you're working with Samuel. I go in to Ocho Rios. Visit the hotels, get acquainted with the managers. I've got to go to Kingston soon. Maybe you'd like to go with me."

"Maybe."

"Anyway—I write at night—after I leave you."

"You're not getting enough sleep. You look peaked around the edges."

"That's your fault."

"Do tell?"

"You're wearing me to a frazzle."

"Maybe you'd better take a hiatus."

"Fat chance. I'll stay with you until I'm wobbly. A derelict wandering up and down the beach with trembling legs and rheumy eyes. And when somebody asks me what happened, I'm going to tell 'em, 'Catherine loved me to death.' "

"You . . ." I burst out laughing and flicked at his crooked nose with my fingernail.

We had such a lovely time that April.

A few days later he said he'd better go to Kingston and he asked if I'd like to come along. When I said yes, he said, "Let's take Samuel. He'd get a kick out of the trip. Will you ask Euphemia if it's O.K.?"

When I asked her she said, "Mistress, Samuel will be tickled for true when I tell him. But you sure he won't be a lot of bother? Maybe Mr. David . . ."

"It was Mister David's idea. And don't worry about Samuel, Euphemia, we'll take good care of him."

"I'm not going to worry, Mistress. Ever since that day you pull those sea urchins out of my boy's foot, I know you going to take care of him no matter what."

"Would you mind looking after Bruce? I know he's a terrible cat, and I hate to ask you, but I don't know what else to do. We'll only be gone a couple of days."

"He won't be no trouble. That boy Moses love that orange cat better'n he loves his brothers. He and old Bruce, they just seem to understand each other."

"He's a strange cat. He's never seemed to like anybody except my dad. But he's certainly taken to Moses."

Euphemia laughed. "They both be mean as snakes. That's why they get along."

On the morning of our departure Samuel arrived dressed in a clean white shirt and short green pants. He carried a large straw bag packed with a change of clothes.

We took our time driving the narrow, climbing road that led us through Fern Gully, cool and dark and damp and green with every variety of fern known to man. Then on to Linstead and Bog Walk. Past pastureland deep in grass and dotted with thickets, rolling gently as it descended to the sea. Several times I asked David to stop while I sketched a particularly lovely view or a group of people.

We stopped to buy hot roasted corn and stayed to talk to the family who sold it to us. I found that I was becoming more and more interested in the Jamaican people, and I knew that I wanted to learn more about them.

Finally we wound our way down from the smoke-blue mountains to the big, noisy, bustling city of Kingston.

David registered. He and Samuel in one room. Me in another. All very proper. And I liked that.

I waited for them in the coffee shop the next morning, watched them come in, and saw the people around me watching them too: a big white man wearing a sport shirt and Levis. A small black boy, side by side, Samuel so close to David that his arm brushed the Levis when he walked. David's hand rested on the small shoulder.

"Good morning," I said.

"Morning, Catherine." He kissed my cheek.

Samuel grinned. "Morning, Mistress Catherine."

David tucked a big white napkin under Samuel's chin.

"That room got two big beds, Mistress Catherine," Samuel said. "*Two big beds.* And they both got pillows. And there's a table and chairs and three lamps and pictures and everything just like a house. And there be a bathroom and another room that you just use to put your clothes in." He took a sip of water. "I never seen a thing like that room."

David left us after breakfast, and Samuel and I started out to see Kingston. And what a lovely adventure it was to explore a new place in the company of a child, to see things through his delighted, seven-year-old eyes.

We bought a basket for Euphemia in Victoria Crafts Market, wandered through the Royal Botanical Hope Gardens, and ate chocolate ice cream cones in the park. When we passed one of the newer, luxury hotels, I said to Samuel, "Let's go see how the rich folks live."

I'm not fond of luxury hotels when I'm in a foreign city. I love them in New York or Cleveland or Miami, but I rather think that's where they belong. I don't want to take New York with me when I'm in Jamaica.

33

We gave the Grand Central Station-sized lobby a fast look and headed for the arcade. I gave Samuel some change and suggested he buy a few comic books while I browsed.

There were lots of small shops: perfume, tobacco, linens, jewelry. I poked my head in for a look, sniffed the perfume shop, and bought a bottle of Jamaican perfume. A curio shop looked interesting. The display window was a nice clutter of small rugs, wood carvings, straw hats, most of them of West Indian design, carved ivory, and paper flowers. I started in. I had my hand on the door when I suddenly stopped.

David stood at the end of the counter. His face was grim. His lips were drawn back into so tight a line that his teeth showed. His hands, doubled into fists, were clenched around a Jamaican's tie, lifting the man almost off his feet—a big man with wide, frightened eyes. He wore a black and white pin-stripe suit and had a golden earring in his right ear. I remember thinking how incongruous a golden earring looked with a pin-stripe suit.

It was the third man in the shop that froze me where I stood.

Whitey Koebler. My God, what was he doing in Jamaica? His white, spatula fingers gripped David's arm. His face was close to David's. His thin mouth snarled words I couldn't hear. His hand shot out and cuffed the Jamaican on the side of his head.

Suddenly he turned and looked toward the door.

Almost in slow motion my hand slid down, and I moved away. Wondering, Wondering.

When David returned to the hotel later that afternoon, Samuel and I were sitting on the patio. I looked up and saw him coming toward us. His steps were precise, one careful step at a time, slow and deliberate. He carried a bright orange beach ball.

When he passed a waiter I heard him say, "Two Planters Punch."

He stopped in front of me and looked down into my eyes. "Hi, my love," he said. "Hi, my lovely Catherine-with-a-C."

I took the orange ball out of his hands and tossed it to Samuel. "I want to talk to David," I told him. "Could you play alone for a minute?"

"Sure, Mistress. You holler when you want me."

I watched him bounce away. I didn't want to look at David.

"Drink up," David said.

"I'm not very thirsty."

"Then I'll have to do the drinking for both of us." His voice was slurred. "What's the matter with you, babe?"

"I saw you this afternoon. In the craft shop, I saw you trying to choke that big Jamaican." I swallowed and tried to steady my voice. "I saw Whitey Koebler."

"Whitey . . . ! How in the hell . . . ?"

"I met him at a party at Mary's. Just before I came to Jamaica. I took this assignment partly because of him."

"Just what in the hell are you talking about?"

"I met him at Mary's," I repeated. "That night, later, he called. He didn't give his name, but I knew who it was." I sat forward in my chair. "He said, quite calmly I remember, that he wanted to screw me."

David's face looked white and still.

"And then he called back and he said he wanted to hurt me with his hands. He wanted to . . ." I couldn't go on. I tried to pick up one of the drinks, but my hands were shaking so badly I couldn't manage the glass.

"Jesus," David said. He closed his eyes.

"And now he's here. He's a friend of yours."

"He's not a friend of mine."

"How could you . . . ?"

35

His hand covered mine. Stopping me. "I'm going to tell you something," he said. "A few years ago, three to be exact, I worked for the government."

"But you're a travel writer. You told me . . ."

"I *am* a travel writer. I always have been. When you're doing the kind of work I did, you need a cover. Travel writing is a perfect cover. A lot of travel writers do the same thing I did." He took a long pull at his drink.

"You mean you were some kind of an agent?"

"Narcotics. Let me explain it to you, Catherine. A travel writer is free to move around. He's got a good reason to be wherever he is. If, for instance, I had a job in . . . well, say, Mexico City, I could go and nobody would suspect anything. I'd be there to cover the opening of a new hotel or maybe the bullfight season."

"Is that why you're here? Are you . . . ?"

"You're not listening, babe. I said I left the government three years ago. I'm strictly a travel writer now."

"Thank goodness."

"Why 'thank goodness?' "

"I don't know, David. I guess because the business of undercover men has always struck me as being cops-a-robberish."

He frowned.

"Darling, I know somebody has to do it. I don't have any sympathy for people who break the law, especially for people who deal in drugs, and I know there have to be strong law enforcement agencies. It's just that I'm glad you're out of it."

"Well, I am."

"And what about this afternoon? Maybe it's not any of my business, but I can't imagine you associating with a man like Whitey."

"That's why I wanted to explain the kind of work I used to

do. When I was doing it, Catherine, I met a lot of bums—hoods, pushers, hit men, torch men, informers. I've known Whitey for a lot of years." He took another long pull at his drink.

"He's been mixed up in every kind of racket known to man. But when I first knew him, he was a stick man in Vegas and he was living with an ex-hooker."

He looked at me over the rim of his glass. "Maybe I shouldn't tell you this. I don't want to scare you, but I want you to know what kind of a guy he is. You're right to be afraid of him. He's a vicious, amoral animal." His hand tightened around his glass. "This girl he was living with, the ex-hooker, she was a pretty little thing, and I think she really liked Whitey. But a hooker's a hooker. They can never resist a fast twenty bucks. Anyway, Whitey got suspicious. He began to watch her, and one afternoon he had somebody stand in for him at the table and he went back to their apartment. The girl was there with a john."

He sighed deeply. "The john got out, but the girl didn't. He sliced up her breasts."

I remember the coldness of the man's gray eyes, the fish-belly color of his pale skin. I remembered the way he had looked at me that night at Mary's. And the sound of his voice on the phone.

"He got out of Vegas one step ahead of the cops and headed for Cuba," David went on. "He worked in the casinos there until Castro took over and closed them." He put his hand on my hair. "Why didn't you tell me about the phone calls before?"

"I wanted to forget them. I know a lot of women get unpleasant phone calls occasionally. I told myself he was just a creep I'd never have to see again. I didn't tell Mary about the calls either. I just said I thought he was a weird character and

I hoped she wasn't going to see him again. And I don't think she will. She's got a new boyfriend, and she'll be busy with him. So there didn't seem to be any reason to tell you or anybody else. But now, to have him turn up here, to have him be somebody you know . . ." I could hear the edge of hysteria in my own voice.

David gripped my hands. "He won't bother you again."

"What about you? Are you going to see him?"

He shook his head. "He'll be going back to New York in a day or two."

"Are you sure? What was he doing in Kingston anyway?"

"He owns the curio shop you saw today."

"But if he owns the shop, he must live here."

"He never stays around for long. Franklin, the black guy you saw today, he handles things at the shop."

"And what about him? You looked . . . I thought you were going to kill him."

"He's just a punk, Catherine. He said something about my kid, about Davey. I couldn't help myself. I wanted to kill him." He pushed his chair back. "I want you to forget it. And about that other business too. I'm just a travel writer now, babe. A travel writer who got lucky and came to Jamaica and met a beautiful woman and a damn fine kid. And I think it's time we did the town, because we're heading back to Ocho Rios tomorrow."

"It's going to rain, sport. Don't you think we ought to stick around the hotel?"

"To hell with the rain." He leaned over suddenly and kissed me. "I'm sorry about what happened today, my love. Sorry you saw me with that bastard. But he's got nothing to do with us. I'm going to take care of you, Catherine, and you'll never have to be frightened of him or anybody else again." He took his jacket off and placed it around my shoulders. "To shelter you from the rain, Mistress Catherine. To shelter you from the rain."

"David . . ." I don't know why. I don't know what it was. But in that moment I could have wept for him.

We looked at each other for a long moment, and then he turned away. "Hey Samuel!" he yelled. "Let's go tell Kingston goodbye." And as he watched Samuel wave in agreement and start toward us, he said to me, "He really is a damned fine kid, isn't he? In some nutty kind of way he reminds me of Davey at that age. A little serious, a little wide-eyed. Boys are such a special breed."

Rain spattered the streets when we came out of the hotel.

"Told you it was going to rain," I said.

He smacked my bottom. "Smart ass," he said. "Lovely ass."

Samuel splashed through puddles ahead of us, as happy as a Spaniel during hunting season.

"He's liable to catch cold," I worried.

"He'll be fine. Tell you what, we'll buy him a new pair of pants."

"I don't need no more pants, Mister David. I already got two pair. One to wash. The other to wear."

"And now you'll have a third. In case you bust your ass out of the other two." He put his hand on Samuel's shoulder and steered him into a store.

Samuel looked embarrassed. "I don't need anything, Mister David," he whispered.

"I know you don't, kid. But it would please me to buy you something." He rubbed the top of Samuel's head and moved him over to the counter. And he said to the clerk, "Madam, we have come out on this rainy day to buy Davey a pair of pants."

Samuel looked startled. "My name is Samuel," he said.

David stared down at him. His face went white. He bit down hard on his lower lip and took a deep breath. The store seemed suddenly quiet.

The woman took out a neat stack of trousers. She selected a pair of black-and-white checked pants and a pair of navy-blue. "These will fit him," she said.

"Fine," David said. His hands were shaking. "We'll take them. And a shirt. A red shirt. And underpants." He bent down and touched Samuel's head. "O.K.? These O.K.?"

Samuel bobbed his head, embarrassed.

"You're wet," David said. "You'll catch cold." He took the clothes. "Give me a dry cloth," he said to the woman. He reached for Samuel. "Come here, boy," he said. And then, kneeling, stripped Samuel to his skin, dried him with the cloth, and began to dress him in the new clothes.

The rain stopped by the time we left the store. Samuel puddle-jumped down the street ahead of us. I glanced at David, and saw that he was following Samuel with his eyes.

"A boy is a wondrous thing," he said. Then, "Aw, what the hell. What the bloody damned hell!"

Rain began to spatter again as we neared the hotel. "Run ahead," I called to Samuel. "Don't get your new clothes wet." I took David's hand. "Come on, David. Come on. Let's get out of the rain."

"A wondrous thing," he said. "A wondrous thing."

He let go of my hand and swung himself around a sign pole. Water poured down from a broken gutter. He turned his face up to the water spout and let it wash over him.

I put my hand on his shoulder. "Darling," I said. "Darling, come out of the rain."

CHAPTER FIVE

A white Mercedes with a rental license plate was parked in the driveway to the beach house. "Looks like we've got company," I said.

Euphemia appeared at the door and waved. She hurried over to pick Samuel up in her arms for a hug. Over his shoulder she said, "Mistress Mary be here. With two gentlemen and two ladies."

I took David's hand and said, "Come on, you'll want to meet her."

"Listen, maybe Samuel and I will go take a swim."

"No you don't. You're not running out on me."

I squeezed his hand. "We haven't had a chance to talk. There are still so many things I want to ask you."

He looked at me quizzically. "Are you still worrying about Whitey?"

I wanted to tell him that, no, I had forgotten the scene in the curio shop. I wanted to, but I couldn't. "I guess I can't really understand why you'd even be civil to him," I said.

"We'll talk about it later if you want to. But much later. I'm going to have other things on my mind if I ever get you alone. Do you realize I haven't really kissed you in four days? Samuel is a hell of a fine kid, and I enjoyed having him along, but it's time I was alone with my girl."

"We'll break away," I promised. "One quick drink and I'll make some excuse."

His hands were on my shoulders. "Tell them we've got a dinner date." His hands tightened, hurting my shoulders. "Jesus, Catherine," he said. "I want you. Right now. I'd like to take you behind one of those sand dunes and . . ."

"Darling," Mary shrieked, exploding into the room I like a well dressed firecracker. "You've come at last." She threw her arms around me and kiss-kissed my cheek while she eyed David.

"This is David," I said. "David McKenna. Mary Bernardi."

"How nice," she said. She stared up at him, touched manicured fingernails to her smart Sasson hair, pursed her lips, and said, "You're a tough-looking son-of-a-bitch."

He put his hand out. "It takes one to know one," he said.

Her eyes widened. Then she laughed. "Darling," she said, not looking at me, "wherever did you find him?"

"I won him in a raffle," I said sweetly.

Kitty and Laura and Mark were there too. A nice surprise. I hadn't expected them to come with Mary. I hugged the women and turned my cheek for Mark's kiss. When I stepped away from him I saw Alan Carlisle lounging at the edge of the terrace. When he came toward me Mary said, "You remember Alan, darling." Her voice sounded breathless. And I thought, so she has taken him as her lover.

I said, "Of course. Hello. It's nice to see you again. This is David. David McKenna."

They shook hands. And for no reason that I could fathom, it seemed to me they looked each other over carefully.

"What did you do with the cat?" Alan asked her. "Shoot it?"

"I thought about that," I said. "But I decided a vacation might improve his disposition. I brought him with me."

"How does he like Jamaica?"

"Fine. He's taken a shine to Euphemia's youngest boy.

The kid carries him around like a sack of potatoes, and Bruce loves it."

"Come on, let me get you a drink. Mary will take care of David."

He led me over to the bar, dipped a ladle into a crystal punch bowl, and said:

"One of sour,
Two of sweet,
Three of strong,
Four of weak

"A Planter's Punch for m'lady. I hope you like it."

"Marvelous," I said after I'd sampled it. "Thank you." The cool fruit flavor mixed with rum was delicious. "I didn't expect to see you," I said after my second sip.

"I didn't expect to be here. I was disappointed when you weren't here to meet us. You've just come in from Kingston?"

"Yes, and I'm hot and tired. I'm going out for dinner."

"I don't think so, Cathy. Mary's planning on all of us having dinner together tonight. She'd be upset if you ran out the first night she was here."

He smiled at me over his glass. A mocking, not very nice smile. "Did you like Kingston?"

"No. Well, I mean yes, I suppose I liked *seeing* it. But it was hot and bustling." I shrugged. "I'd rather be here. That's all."

"Get up to the Blue Mountain Inn for dinner?"

"No. Did I miss something?"

"You sure did. Beautiful place. Tucked up in the Blue Mountains. Good food and you get a wonderful view of Kingston. McKenna should have taken you." The mocking smile again. "But I suppose he kept you pretty busy." He took

43

another slow sip of his drink while he watched me with his cool green eyes. "Known him long?"

"Two weeks."

"Well, Kingston's a good place to get better acquainted in. A good place for all sorts of . . . fun and games."

I set my drink down carefully. "I've got to change," I said. "Thanks for the drink."

He looked amused. "Don't be angry. You're old enough for games."

My hands were shaking. I had an unlady-like urge to sock him on his too-perfect nose. I've never been good at handling this sort of thing. All I could do was say, "Excuse me," and beat a retreat. I wondered when I was in the shower why in the world Mary had brought him to Jamaica.

I put on a long, pale yellow, cotton dress, brushed my hair and held it back with a matching yellow scarf. Then I went out to meet my enemy. I remember now that's what I thought . . . I'm dressed to meet my enemy. I don't recall that I ever disliked anyone as much as I disliked Alan Carlisle.

Mary had placed flaming torches on each of the four corners of the terrace. She had her arms through David's, and when I went to join them she said, "I'm not going to let the two of you get away. I've planned a lovely evening, and it won't be lovely if you're not a part of it."

"Well . . ." I started to say, "David thought . . ."

"David's changed his mind, haven't you darling?"

And that, it seemed, was that.

The night was soft. The food was good. The trade winds were just strong enough to make the palms rustle pleasantly. Yes, it was a nice night. But I didn't want to be here. I wanted to be at the hotel, alone with David. I didn't like Alan, and at the moment I wasn't even sure I liked Mary.

David sat next to her. I sat between Laura and Mark. Alan,

next to Kitty, sat opposite me.

"How are the illustrations coming?" Mary asked.

"Fine," I said. "I'm using Euphemia's middle boy. Samuel. He's marvelous. Just the right age. Wonderfully curious. Excited at everything he sees. You should have seen him in Kingston."

"Kingston?" Her drink poised. "You mean you took him to Kingston with you?"

"Yes. He was great fun to have along. He got such a kick out of the room he shared with David. He couldn't get over the size of the beds, and the lamps and pictures, and that there was a room you used just for your clothes." I smiled a slow smile at Alan. "He was lots of fun. Fun and games all the way."

"But why in the world would you want to take a seven-year-old boy when you're going away with a man?" Mary asked.

"How really queer," Kitty laughed.

"But rather nice," Laura put in, smiling at me.

"Yes," Alan said, "rather nice." And I was pleased to see that he had the grace to look embarrassed.

We were drinking coffee when Mary suggested a liqueur. "Alan, darling, bring the liqueur. And some ganja." She clapped her hands together. "We'll get high and have a skinny dip party. It's a marvelous night for it." She turned to David. "All right with you?"

"Sure, it's all right with me. But what's the big deal? Jamaican pot? Probably lousy stuff."

"Top grade," Mary said.

"Maybe you'd rather have something stronger," Alan said.

"Maybe."

"And Cathy?"

"Catherine has no bad habits," David said. "And that's

the way I like her."

Alan reached across the table for my left hand and held it up to the candlelight. "I don't see any rings on her fingers." The mocking grin again. He flicked the palm of my left hand with his fingernail. I couldn't help myself, I winced.

The grin faded. He turned my hand over and touched the palm with his fingertips. "What happened?"

"Sea urchins," I said crossly, trying to retrieve my hand.

"But, Catherine. They're the ugliest creatures in the world. Why in heaven's name would you pick one up?" Mary asked.

"They were stuck on Samuel's feet. I picked two of 'em off him before I thought about it." I tugged my hand away. "And, no thanks on the pot!"

"I went to a party last week," Mark said. "The hostess served a green salad garnished with grass. And a sniff of coke for dessert. Let me tell you, folks, it sure beats apple pie."

"Whose party?" Laura asked.

"Never you mind, sweets. Anyway, you'd never believe me. She always plays a dowager aunt. Not at all the type you'd ever dream would turn on to drugs. I knew youngish boys were her thing—but drugs! She's marvelous. That was the first time I'd ever tried coke, and for me it's the greatest. But more expensive than grass, of course. And the way you feel! Utter euphoria. If you've never tried it, Catherine, you really should. It's trendy, pet, it's the thing to do." He looked hopefully at Mary. "Is it too much to hope for, or do you have a tad of cocaine?"

She looked at Alan. "Do we, darling?"

"I can check the larder," he said.

Laura pushed her chair back. "Forget it!" she snapped. "I don't know about the rest of you, but I didn't come to Jamaica to get stoned. I came to play golf. Isn't there a local nightspot? I'd rather go dancing than sit here and watch everybody bomb out."

"The Jumbalaya," Mary said.

"Let's go," Laura continued. "Alan, what about you?"

"Sorry, I've got an appointment in town."

"But Alan, darling, I wanted all of us to be together tonight," Mary pouted.

"Sorry. Maybe Mark can take you. Or David. Unless he
has other plans too. What about it McKenna? You game to
compete with the local bucks?"

"Not tonight," David said.

"I'll take the girls," Mark said, "if you'll give me a little
something to fortify me on my journey. Although, what I'm
going to do while you-all are making time with the local
dudes, I don't know."

"Find one for yourself," Kitty said. "You don't have any
trouble in New York."

He pursed his lips and chuckled. "All right. But I need
something to speed me on my way."

"Alan will get you something?" Mary said. "Better stick to
ganja tonight."

"Fine. Fine. Thank you, angel. Are you coming?"

"I'm not in the mood. Damn it, anyway, everybody's running out on me. I'd go in and go to bed if I wasn't so keyed up."

"I'll be here, Mary," I said.

"We'll do it another night," David put in. He leaned over
to say something else that I couldn't hear. Something that
made her smile.

And that made her uncomfortable. I got up and went to the
edge of the terrace. The sea was running heavy tonight. I could
see the white foam of the waves and hear the thud and roar
when they hit the shore. And other night noises, Jamaican
night noises. I longed to walk on the beach, to take my shoes
off and feel the sand cool and pliant against my bare feet.

"Like to take a walk?" Alan said.

Startled, feeling as though he'd read my mind, I stared at him for a moment before I snapped, "No."

"Nice night for it." And when I didn't answer he said, "I'm sorry about what I said earlier. About Kingston. I don't know why I said it."

"It's not important." I replied wishing he'd go away. Then in spite of myself, I asked, "What's that sound?"

"Whistling frogs. Sound like midget blacksmiths, don't they?"

"I've never heard them before. Every place has it's own particular night sounds, I suppose."

He nodded. "Trucks rumbling through the streets, horns blowing, heels clicking against the pavement. That's New York. Crickets, whistling frogs, and palms blowing in the wind. Jamaica. Sure you wouldn't like to walk a bit?"

"I thought you were going out."

"There's no hurry." He looked at me. "I tried to phone you in New York. The operator said your number had been changed to an unlisted number."

"That's right. I . . . had a couple of unpleasant phone calls." 'From your friend, Whitey,' I wantd to say, but didn't.

"I was sorry I couldn't see you before you left. I wanted to." He glanced at David. "I suppose now you're more or less involved."

"I suppose I am." My voice was cool.

"Meet him here?"

"Yep. Picked him up on the beach." I said, being deliberately nasty, not knowing quite why.

I turned away from him then with an "Excuse me" and started toward David. He was holding Mary's hand. I heard her say, "Consider this your house, darling."

"Thanks, Mary. Appreciate it. You sure you don't want to go out with the others?"

"No, I'm just going to sit here and listen to the night." She chuckled. "Want to join me?"

She's drunk, I thought.

"Another time," he said.

When we were alone David said, "So much for your friends. You'd met Alan before?"

"Yes, once. At Mary's. The same night I met your friend Whitey. I had the idea they were friends."

His face suddenly looked wary. "What makes you think so?"

"Mary said she met them at a party, so obviously they knew each other. I'm not much fonder of him than I am of Whitey. I'm not fond of anybody that's into drugs. Would you have gone along with the pot-or-whatever bit?"

"I'd have stayed around to see how far it went. Maybe I'm like a retired race horse—I hear the bugle and I'm ready to run. I was a cop so long that I snap to attention when anybody mentions drugs." He was silent for a moment, and then he said, "Alan seems to know where there's a good supply."

"Probably a little sideline of his—running drugs! I can't imagine where in the world Mary found him. And she's got such a gleam in her eye when she looks at him. He's a good twelve years younger than she is."

"And I'm a good twelve years older than you are."

"Yes, but . . . but that's different."

"Is it?"

"Of course it is. Don't you know that? Don't you know how I feel?"

"Yes, Catherine, I know. But I'm not sure you should.

Look, I know every guy who's ever wanted to get a woman really interested in him has said this. But I mean it. I'm not sure you should. I'm a beat-up guy who's been over the road a few thousand times. The thing with Davey—not knowing where he is or what he might be going through—took a hell of a lot out of me. I'm not what I'd like to be for you."

I leaned into him. "You're fine for me," I said. "Just the way you are, beat-up, crooked nose and all."

He folded his arms around me. "I don't think I remembered to tell you that I love you," he whispered into my hair. Then he held me away from him and said, "Now I'm going to send you back up to the house. Say goodnight nicely and lock your door."

"Say goodnight nicely?"

"That's what I said."

"To you too?"

"Yep."

"So what happened to all that lovely lust among the dunes? Change your mind?"

He looked startled. Then he laughed. "Jesus," he said. "Sometimes you surprise me." He pulled me against him and swatted my fanny. "I have a feeling tonight is not the night. The whole evening was a little off. And that green-eyed son-of-a-bitch set my teeth on edge."

"Mine too. Now I've got a double reason for disliking him." I sighed. "You afraid of a little sand, are you?"

"Will you shut up? Listen, I may have to run into town in the morning, so I probably won't see you on the beach. I'll catch up with you later." His hands circled my waist. "I'll take a raincheck on the sand dune. And when I do, it'll be so great we'll scare the fish,"

"Promises. Promises."

"And remember to lock your door tonight. I didn't like the

way that guy looked at you, and I've got a feeling he walks in his sleep."

"I bet he's not allergic to sand." When he started towards me I laughed and scooted up the dune to the house.

Mary was alone on the terrace when I returned, breathless from my run up to the house. "You want to talk a while or are you ready for bed?" I asked her.

"Ready for almost anything." She smiled. A vague, distant smile.

"Mary?"

I put my hand on her shoulder.

Her body swayed.

"What's the matter with you?"

"Happy, happy," she said.

"Did you take something?" I shook her. "Did Alan give you something?"

"Alan's good to me, Catherine. So goooooooood . . ."

Damn! I didn't know anything about drugs. I didn't know how to handle this. If only David were still here. I tried again, "Mary, what did he give you?"

She put her fingers to her lips, cautioning me. "Shhhh. Shhhh, or you won't hear."

"Hear what?"'

"Secrets."

"What secrets?"

"The palm trees are telling secrets. If you listen very carefully, you'll hear . . ." Her voice trailed off to a whisper.

"Where's Alan? Is he still here?"

"Gone. Some men came and he went with them. Big, dark Jamaican men."

"Let's go to bed, Mary."

"No! I have to stay here. I have to listen to the secrets."

"We'll listen tomorrow. Now it's time for bed." I pulled

her to her feet and walked her to her bedroom.

"Silly Catherine." Her voice was a sing-song. "Silly Catherine doesn't know what she's missing. What a lovely, lovely feeling. What a . . ."

After she fell asleep I went down the long quiet hall to my room, feeling the chill of the night as I had never felt it before.

At 3:15 I heard Alan's footsteps coming down the hall. They stopped outside my door. I held my breath until they moved on.

It was a long time before I was able to sleep.

CHAPTER SIX

I worked with Samuel until noon the next day. When he left, I put my sketch pad away and reached into the cooler for a cold can of Red Stripe, the local beer. I took a long, cool sip and stared out at the turquoise sea. I tried to relax, tried to forget the night before.

Finally I smoothed the blanket out and lay down, shading my eyes with my arm, willing myself to doze.

I wondered about the drug. What kind of a drug Alan had given her. How frightening it must be to be so out of yourself. And why did people take drugs anyway? I knew so little about them. Then I remembered Jenny.

We had been neighbors when I first came to New York three years ago—neighbors, and then friends, in spite of the difference in our ages, for Jenny was seventeen and I was twenty-four. Her husband was a little older than she was. I only saw him a few times before he left her. She rarely talked about him. Most of our conversations were about her child, a nine-month-old girl whose name was Annie.

"I want such good things for her," I remember Jenny saying. "I don't want her to be like me." And then. "I took drugs."

"Like marijuana?"

She smiled at me. Patiently she listed on her fingers, "Marijuana, coke, hash, reds, yellows, blues, L.S.D., heroin."

"But how . . . how could you afford all those things? Heroin. Isn't heroin an expensive habit?"

"Ya. Well . . . like I promised guys I'd put out, but then I didn't."

Even I knew the world does not work that way.

Once she said, "I used to act. In some off-Broadway things. When I was thirteen and fourteen. I was really good. Everybody said I was really good. Want to see a picture of me?"

She rummaged through a cardboard box, through old theatre programs, hair clips, a baby's pacifier, notebooks, a blue sock, five or six photographs, and at last she said, "Here it is. I was fourteen. See how pretty I was when I was young?"

'See how pretty I was when I was young.'

The words stayed with me a long time. Long after Jenny moved away.

And it was men like Alan who supplied children like Jenny.

There was a part of the world that I knew very little about. Certainly I didn't know about men like Alan. Or Whitey.

And the words. Hookers, pushers, johns, hitmen, stickmen, joints, hash, coke. All foreign to me. A different world. It had been David's world.

Wouldn't it be nice before you fell in love to be able to decide exactly what type of man he would be? Short or tall, thin or fat. One who would rather go to a concert than a football game. Who'd rather read Snoopy and Peanuts instead of Dick Tracy. And as to his profession, wouldn't it be nice to say, "I'll fall in love with a bus driver. Or a teacher. Or a tree surgeon." But it doesn't work that way. Unfortunately.

Why couldn't David have been a tree surgeon?

I raised my head and took a sip of beer. It was hot. I was hot. Groggy. Tired. Tired from all the thoughts jumping like jacks inside my head. I got up and went toward the water, shaking my head to clear it.

The water felt stinging cool against my ankles. A wind had come up, and the waves splashed to my hips. I went farther out, jumping high when a giant wave rolled in, almost knocking me off my feet. But feeling good now. Feeling refreshed. Ready when the next wave hit, diving through it, swimming out the other side.

Straight out. And as I swam I seemed to leave my preoccupations back on the shore. Now there was just the blue-gray sky overhead and the water, the lovely cool water caressing my skin as gently as a lover.

The wind picked up, and I found myself having to swim harder. The sun disappeared behind a cloud, turning the turquoise water an ominous gray. I started back, surprised at how far I'd come. The waves were higher. For every yard forward I was thrown a yard back.

"Well, Catherine," I told myself, "you've been foolish. But you're going to be O.K. if you keep cool. Just swim steady, one good stroke at a time, don't think about JAWS. Breathe slowly, and you're going to be fine. Scared but fine. That's it. Stroke, stroke, stroke. Easy does it. Easy does . . ." I swallowed a mouthful of water, gagged, and went under.

When my head bobbed to the surface I gulped for air. "Calm down," the voice inside my head ordered. But the voice wasn't calm. It had a frantic, frightened edge to it. "You're O.K. Don't panic. Don't panic!"

A large wave caught me and hurled me forward and down. Down, down, down. Opening my eyes, down here it was still turquoise. Curiously calmer. Curiously pretty.

My lungs were bursting for air. I struggled up. Push, push. Head above the water. But tired. Oh, so tired.

And cold. Chills racking my body, making it almost impossible to swim. Waves washing over me. Pushing me under. Warmer under the water. A soft, turquoise warmth. Not so bad after all. Just . . . let . . . it . . . all . . . go. Just . . . let . . . it . . .

Something was pulling my hair. I wanted to say, "Stop it! Stop it right now!"

Sputtering. Choking. A hand clutching my hair. An arm under my shoulders.

"It's all right, Cathy. I've got you."

I shook my head and pawed the hair out of my face.

"I'll get you in."

Trying to see him. Trying to see through turquoise filled eyes.

I gagged when the waves splashed over my face. Panic again. I held to him, my arms tight around his neck. He tore my fingers away and slapped me, hard.

On my back. Gray sky. Gray waves. Gray rain. The sound of thunder. And of his breath rasping in his throat.

Then he was standing, pulling me along with him, half carrying, half dragging me. I felt sand beneath my feet. His arm was around me. Then I was out of the water, blinded by rain, falling to my knees. Flat on my stomach, my face turned sideways. Being lifted from my waist. Pulling, pushing. Water running out of my mouth. Again and again. Finally, with a cough and a sputter, I pushed his hands away and rolled over.

Alan's lips were white against his tanned face. "You're all right, Cathy. You're all right now."

"Where did you come from? How did you . . ."

"I took a walk. Then I saw you. I saw you disappear." His face was grim, taut. "That was a stupid thing to do. In a storm. Any time. To swim out so far alone."

"The storm hadn't hit. I didn't realize. I was thinking and swimming, and then when I started back it just suddenly . . ." I hugged myself. "I was so frightened."

Even now. So frightened I wanted to howl, wanted to lean against him. Wanted to feel the warmth of somebody after the awful coldness of the water and now the coldness of the rain. But I remembered last night.

"I'm O.K." I said, trying to sound brisk. I stood up. But damn! It's hard to sound brisk when your teeth are chattering and rain is dripping off your nose.

"You are shivering." He picked up a towel and tried to dry me. "Better?"

"S . . . sure." I was shaking so hard I could hardly stand. He pulled me to him trying to warm me with his body.

I started to cry. I hated myself for crying. But I couldn't stop. I sobbed and snorted and gulped and yowled. Remembering my terror. Remembering the sea closing in around me. Lightning split the sky in pieces, and I clung to him.

His arms tightened. "It's all right, Cathy. I'll take you home now."

Finally I shuddered to a stop. "Thanks, Alan," I managed to say. "There's no way to say it adequately. Just, thank you. You saved my life."

"You can do the same for me some day. Now let's get you back and have Mary get some hot coffee into you."

Again I remembered last night. "I doubt that Mary is in any condition to take care of herself, let alone me." I said the words with careful precision, a little sad that I had to say them.

"What do you mean?"

"You don't know? Come on, Alan."

"Know what?"

"Last night. She was spaced out. Is that the right word? She was spaced out on whatever you gave her before you left. Is that why she brought you along? To keep her well supplied?"

"What in the hell are you talking about?"

"When I came back from the beach Mary was out of it.

Listening to the palm trees telling secrets! I'm sorry. I shouldn't say anything. Not now. Not after what you've done. But I can't help it. You talked about drugs last night. You . . ."

"So you think I gave her a drug." His green eyes shot sudden sparks of anger.

"Didn't you?"

He just looked at me. Then he went down and picked up my things. "Let's get you back to the house."

"Alan . . ."

"Skip it, Cathy. Let's skip it."

I moved away from him. When I did, my legs folded beneath me and I sank to the sand, feeling foolish and weak.

He looked down at me. He handed me my things, then bent down and lifted me up in his arms.

We didn't speak all the way up the beach.

When we got to the house, Mary and the others were in the living room. Euphemia was serving drinks.

When she saw us, Mary got to her feet, her hands on her hips. She said, "How sweet! Were you playing house out in the rain?"

Alan looked past her to Euphemia. "Miss Catherine almost drowned," he said. "She needs a hot bath and some tea. Will you help her, please?" He put me down.

"Yes Sir, Mister Alan."

She put her arm around me. "You come along, Mistress. You're going to feel better, soon as you drink some hot tea."

"Catherine, I'm sorry," Mary said. "Is there anything I can do? What happened? Are you sure you're all right?"

"Yes, I'm all right now." My teeth were chattering. "I just feel like I'll never get warm. Maybe a bath . . ."

Laura threw her arms around me. "Don't you want a drink? Maybe some brandy?"

"No, she doesn't want a drink," Alan said. "She wants a bath." The mocking smile. "And she wants David. Don't you, Cathy?"

"Yes, I want David."

"I'll phone him for you."

"Thank you."

"My pleasure."

I had the bath and the tea, and then I slept for a long time. I dreamed of turquoise water, of silvery fish, of seaweed, and of a man with a mocking smile. When I woke David was sitting beside me.

CHAPTER SEVEN

In the warm comfort of David's arms I could close my eyes and let all the fright ooze out of me, safe now with my face against his shoulder.

"My God," he said over and over. "When Alan called me . . ."

"But it's all right now."

"It was a damn stupid thing to do, Catherine."

"I know. That's what Alan told me too." I sighed. "I hate to be so grateful to someone I dislike as much as I dislike him."

"I'm grateful too. Now let's forget him."

I remember that evening with David as one of the last happy times. We sat together on the bed, looking out at the sand and the palms, touching and close. I remember the tenderness in his eyes. We didn't talk much. Just being with him was enough.

No one bothered us until Euphemia knocked and entered with a tray. "I brought your dinner, Mistress. For you and Mr. David. Miss Mary say you eat here and that she will come in later. She thought tonight you like to be alone."

"She thought right," David, said. He took the tray while Euphemia cleared the table in front of the French doors. "You glad to have Samuel back?"

"Yes sir. You think, with eleven boys, I wouldn't even notice when one of them's gone. But I do. I miss them plenty. I knew Samuel was just fine with you and Mistress Catherine. But I missed him. People say it's not good to have so many children and maybe they be right. But I look at my boys and I ask myself, 'Euphemia, if you had to take away six of them, which six would you have not had?' And I can never answer. We have a hard time getting along, but they be good boys and they help all they can. Tomorrow night there's going to be a ship in. All the boys be going to work loading bananas."

"Samuel too?" I asked.

She nodded.

"He's awfully young."

"I know, Mistress. But there's things he can do. He can run errands, carry messages, gather up smaller broken stalks. All the children be working. He say next year he be able to tote a whole hand of bananas himself."

"I'd kind of like to watch one of those ships being loaded," David said.

"Lots of tourist folks go. You go on over to the loading sheds tomorrow night. They be working and loading all night. You maybe go too, Mistress. Now you eat your dinner and then you rest, and tomorrow you be fine."

"I'm glad Mary thought of this," David said after Euphemia had gone. "I don't feel like facing a crowd tonight. And I know you're not up to it."

"I didn't think Mary would be up to it either."

"Oh? Why?"

I hesitated. Then I told him about Mary, about how she'd acted the night before, and that I was sure Alan had given her something. I felt a twinge of guilt, implicating Alan, but it was only David I was telling. And if Alan was involved in drugs, then David should know.

"I've never seen anybody act like that," I said. "She didn't even know her own name. She was out of it. Humming, listening to the palm trees talk!"

He frowned. "Don't exaggerate, Catherine. I'm sure it wasn't all that bad. Did she say anything that made any sense?"

"Not much. She said that Alan made her feel good. I'm sure he gave her something. And I'm not exaggerating, David. She *was* stoned!"

"O.K., O.K., I'll keep an eye on Alan. Now eat your dinner, and when you've finished, I'm going to put you to bed and say a Jamaican farewell."

"I wish we could be together tonight."

"So do I. But not here."

"It's just that I still feel . . . I was terribly frightened, David. And then I seemed to want to let go. To just drift down and down . . ."

He grabbed me and held me close. "God, Catherine," he said. "God, if anything happened to you . . ."

I leaned down and cradled his head, smoothing the shaggy salt and pepper hair with my fingers. "But it didn't, darling. Don't think about it. And I won't either. I promise you."

We stayed like that for a long time. I didn't want him to leave, but after we'd eaten he kissed me, and left. I watched him as he went out through the French doors, across the patio, and down to the beach. I smiled, as I had that first morning, at his lumbering policeman's walk. And I wondered if perhaps he'd been lying to me that day in Kingston. He had to give me an explanation that day. Perhaps the easiest way out was to tell me a half-truth, that he'd been an agent in the past, but that he no longer was one. I wasn't sure how I'd feel if I learned the truth. Keep right on loving him, I supposed.

Mary came in after he left. And she was like the Mary I'd always known. A little flighty, a little silly even, but so nice.

So dear. I tried to forget the night before. I tried to forget what she said when she saw Alan and me together. And I knew, in her way, she was sorry. She came over and sat on the side of the bed and took my hand.

"Feeling better, darling?"

"Yes, I'm fine."

"I never would forgive myself if anything had happened to you."

"But nothing did. And if it had, it wouldn't have been your fault."

"But I'm the one who insisted you come to Jamaica."

I squeezed her hand. "And you were right. Jamaica has been good for me. I can think about dad now without dissolving into tears—think about the good years and not dwell on the sadness and the pain. I can even think of Isabel without grinding my teeth. So you were right, pal, I needed a change of scene. And I think I'm doing a good job on the illustrations. Do you like them? Have I caught what you wanted? It's such a good story that I want the illustrations to be good."

"They're wonderful. Exactly what I wanted. You were right to choose Samuel; he's a perfect *Island Boy.*" She smiled down at me. "So, after all, you're glad that you came?"

"More than glad, Mary. And just think, if I hadn't, I wouldn't have met David."

"You really like him, don't you?"

"More than like."

"Love?"

"You got it!"

She leaned down and kissed my cheek. "I'm so glad, Catherine. I want all the best there is for you. Now—the girls want to see you. All right if they come in for a minute?"

"Of course. I'm not sick. Just a little damp around the edges."

Laura had been crying. "Hey," I said, "what's the matter?"

"You. When I think that you almost . . ." Her eyes filled.

"But I didn't. I just did something terribly foolish that I will never, never do again. And no harm's been done. It turned out all right."

"It wouldn't have if Alan didn't come along."

"But Alan did come along," he said from the door.

"And thank God you did," Kitty said.

"Could you have made it alone?" Mark asked.

I looked across the room at Alan. "No," I said. "I couldn't have made it alone." And then, to change the subject, I said, "Hey, want to see the banana boats tomorrow night? Euphemia said a ship will be in. David wants to go. And I'd like to make some sketches. What do you think?"

"I don't know," Kitty said. "All those natives! Do you think it's safe?"

Alan laughed. "Kitty, believe me. You'll be a hundred times safer here than you'd be walking down Park Avenue in New York."

"It'll be fun," Mary said. "We'll have dinner here and then go over about ten. All right with you, Alan?"

"For dinner. I've got an appointment later. No bananas for me."

And where do you go, Alan Carlisle? I wondered. Where do you go at night?

"Maybe we could do a few native spots later," Laura said. "Let's make a night of it."

When Mary saw that I was tired, she told them to say good-night, that I had to get some rest. She kissed me. When she did, she leaned over and said, "You know how fond I am of you, darling. I'm a bitch sometimes, but I do love you. And besides, you're the best damned illustrator in New York. I'd hate to lose you." Her eyes filled.

I hugged her. "Friends through whatever, Mary," I said.

Alan, who'd been leaning on the door, moved aside to let them pass. When they were gone, he came over to stand beside the bed. "You're all right?"

"Yes. Thanks. And thanks for today. If you hadn't . . ."

And suddenly with the words it was all back again. I pulled the sheet up under my chin and bit my lip. "Damn," I whispered. "Damn, damn, damn."

He sat on the edge of the bed. "You're entitled to be scared, you know. But it's over now. And tomorrow morning, just to prove you're all right, you and I are going for a swim."

"Oh, no. No way."

"We're going for a swim," he went on, "because if you don't go back in the water right away, you're going to be afraid for a long time. Now try to sleep, and if you can't and you want somebody to talk to, I'm just down the hall. I'll tell you the story of my life, or we'll play gin. Is it the East Indians or the Chinese who say that if you save a life that person is your responsibility? It looks like I'm stuck with you."

He was a difficult man to dislike. And I told him so. "I'm having a hard time figuring you out," I said. "One minute I like you, and the next minute I . . ."

"Go on."

I shook my head.

"You don't like me."

"I didn't say that."

"You didn't have to. We started off wrong from the moment we met. I wish . . ." He cleared his throat. "Look, I'll knock on your door at nine."

"But I don't want to go swimming!"

"You don't want to, but you're going to."

"No, I'm not!"

"Good night, Cathy."

"I'm not going swimming," I shouted at his retreating back.

It was a Jamaican morning that looked like the front page of a travel brochure. Sun coming up strong over the blue-misted mountains, drying the dew from the tulip trees, sparking the hibiscus into bloom. Sandpipers skittering along the sand. Sea birds gliding low over a blessedly calm sea.

First we jogged. I wanted to tell him I didn't need to warm up. That I'd like to have the damn swim and get it over with. But I said, fine, and started up the beach at a good clip.

He kept an easy pace beside me, and I thanked heaven that I'd jogged at least three mornings a week in the park near my apartment. Jogging is a hazardous pleasure in New York, where you jog with one eye on the bushes in front of you and one eye swiveled behind you. So, in spite of myself, I enjoyed the freedom of this Jamaican beach. But I wished it was David lumbering beside me instead of Alan—who didn't lumber, of course.

At last we slowed to a walk. When we regained our breaths, he said, "Ready for that swim?"

I glanced back at the house. I could barely see it over the rise of the dune. "Not here. Let's swim on our own beach."

"Whatever you say. You feel all right this morning?"

"Fine."

"Sleep O.K.?"

"Sure," I lied.

He took my hand when we started into the water. I pulled it away. "Listen," I said, "I'm all right." A wave rolled in and hit me in the face. I started back toward the shore.

"Cathy." His voice was a command.

I stopped.

"Give me your hand."

"Maybe I can do it tomorrow."

His hand circled my wrist. His other hand went around my waist. "I've got you," he said.

We walked together toward the line that separated sea and sky. I tried to fight my rising panic. His hold on me was firm.

When another wave rolled in he said, "Now," and released me.

I closed my eyes against my terror—but in spite of myself I responded. I drove through the wave and came out on the other side, my face in the sun, swimming strongly.

We swam side by side, parallel to the beach, for a long time. Until at last, tired, I rolled onto my back and floated, watching the clouds. "I wonder if clouds float in the sky like we float in the sea," I mused aloud.

"Only their sea is blue, not green."

"The sea isn't green," I said. "It's turquoise. Way down deep where the seaweed grows it's a lovely, cool turquoise."

"Cathy?"

I rolled onto my side. "Race you in," I said.

I swam as hard as I could, leaving behind the thoughts I had a moment ago. Feeling my feet touch bottom, I stood up to run, stumbling in my haste.

His hands reached out to catch me, hands that were wet and slick against my skin, hands that moved up the sides of my body, pulling me to him, his body hard and wet against mine.

I felt him trembling. "I was afraid too," he whispered. "There was a minute, just before I touched the bottom, when I didn't think we could make it. And I thought, I'll just fold my arms around her and we'll rest together. We'll sink into the deep nothingness of the sea and maybe, together, it won't be so bad."

"Alan? . . ."

"Now I keep wanting to touch you and know you're safe. I want to . . . Cathy, I want to . . ."

I tasted the salt on his lips. The warmth of his mouth. Heaven help me, I *wanted* him to kiss me, wanted to feel his long, lean body against mine. We'd beat on old devil death. This was our proof, standing here like this with the sand beneath our feet and the sun hot on our backs. Feeling our bodies grow warm and desire sting our nerve-ends. Feeling, oh God, so beautifully aware of everything around us.

"I guess that proves we're alive," he said when he let me go. The mocking grin was back.

"I guess it does," I said carefully.

"You go on up to the house. I'll be along in a few minutes. Think I'll take another turn. It's a good morning for it."

"Yes," I said, feeling my breath catch in my throat. "Yes, it's a good morning for it."

CHAPTER EIGHT

We lingered over dinner. It was after eleven before we got to the docks. The street leading to the water was crowded with cars, trucks, and people. When we went into the giant warehouse, I could see, far at the end, a big white ship against the pier.

Dozens of trucks loaded with bananas were parked inside the warehouse. The drivers shouted and honked their horns, jockeying for a place amid the mass of people. So many people, all rushing, all running back and forth amid the incessant hum of hundreds of voices. Here and there a snatch of a song. Laughter.

Up to the trucks the men and women went, each one bracing himself when the man on the back of the truck heaved a hand of bananas over the waiting shoulder. The whoofing sound of a grunt, a slight staggering under the weight, then the back straightened. The tally clerk kept a tally of each stem as the line passed along the wharf. He rang a bell and gave each loader a metal token which the loader would later exchange for money.

"Hurry on," he called. "Hurry on."

Voices chanted.

"Come Missa Tallyman, come tally me banana
Day dah light, an' me wan' go home.
Six han', seven han', eight han', bunch!
Day dah light, an' me wan' go home."

★ ★ ★ ★ ★

I began to sketch.

Across the giant warehouse they went then, shouldering against those who'd deposited their load and were on their way back for another. Through the warehouse onto the wharf, up the gangplank of the ship, then disappearing somewhere into its bowels.

"This is like nothing I've ever seen," David said. "In the old days Jamaica supplied the United States, Canada, and Europe with bananas. They slowed down after World War II. Then the 1951 hurricane almost wiped the banana plantations out. But it's still a major industry, and it's the way most of the people make their living."

"Well, it's indecent," Kitty said.

"It's a way of life," he said.

Twelve o'clock. One o'clock. Seat smells. The pace slower now. Faces gray with fatigue. An old woman slumped against a pole, mouth open gulping for air. A skinny old man sleeping against a cart, his legs sprawled out in front of him. The splayed feet of women. A pregnant girl staggering under the weight of the bananas. A young boy falling under the weight, laughing, embarrassed, getting to his feet. A mother stopped to nurse her baby, then handed him to another child.

I stood to one side, out of the way, sketching, trying not to think about what I was recording. It was a way of life, David had said. And life could be hard.

The voices were slower now as they chanted:

"Come Missa Tallyman, come tally me banana.
Day dah light, an' me wan' go home."

They moved slower. Their eyes were vacant with fatigue. Still the truck loads of bananas came.

At 1:30 Kitty, Laura, and Mary said they'd had enough. "I'll never get the smell of this place out of my nostrils," Mary said. "I'm thirsty. I want a drink."

"A tall, cold, strong drink," Kitty said. Her white curls had lost their bounce.

"I'd like to stay," I said. "I want to find Samuel. Everything he does is part of your story of *Island* Boy, Mary. All of this," I gestured with my hand, taking in the giant warehouse, "the bananas, the ship, the warehouse, all part of his life. The smells and the grunts and the songs are Jamaica too."

"You're right, darling, but I've had all the smells I can take for one night. You stay, if you want to."

"Sure, Catherine," David said. "We'll hang around as long as you like."

"Well, come on then, Mark. Let's find a place to have a drink," Mary said.

"The Jumbalaya," Kitty said. "You'll love it, Mary."

"I doubt that, darling, but any place has to be better than this." She gave me a brief hug, warned David to take good care of me, and led the others out to the street.

"Look at their faces," David said. "You could color fatigue gray, couldn't you?"

"This kind of fatigue you could," I answered. "It's their feet that bother me the most. Splayed, worn-out feet, flattened by the sheer weight of what they carry." I sighed. "And the pregnant women. And the old people. I know this is the way a lot of them make their living, but it hurts me to see this kind of back-breaking work. Once in Spain I went into a cathedral that was being remodeled. There were four women on their hands and knees scrubbing every inch of the stone floor. That night, after I'd gone to bed, I could still hear the sound of their scrub brushes."

"Life comes so easily for some and so damn hard for others," he said. "Let's go find our boy."

How to find one small black child among hundreds of others?

"Let's move farther down," David suggested. "Maybe we'll spot him if we move around."

We found a man with a wheelbarrow filled with cokes. Warm cokes. But they were wet and they were good. And we found a wall to lean against.

"Tired, Catherine?"

"Yes, but I want to stay."

"Maybe you should have rested tonight. After yesterday . . ."

"Let's not talk about that again."

"Where's Alan tonight? Why didn't he come?"

"He told Mary he had to meet somebody in town. Every time she wants him to go somewhere he has an appointment. She's not too happy about it."

"I have a funny feeling about him, something that doesn't ring true. Did Mary ever say what he does for a living?"

I shook my head. "No, she's never said. He seems to have all the time in the world. I don't think he's ever mentioned a job."

"Catherine, I'm going to ask you to do something for me. Just . . . keep your eyes open. If you see anything odd, or if he has any visitors . . . You know what I mean?"

"Not exactly." I knew, but I didn't like it.

"Anything unusual. You tell me."

"But David . . ."

"What?"

I didn't want to spy on Alan. I told myself that my reluctance had nothing to do with this morning.

I hadn't told David about my swim. In fact, I'd spent all day trying not to think about it.

I'd gone swimming with Alan because I'd known he was

right. It was better to face my fear and get it over with. And it hadn't been so bad—not with him beside me. Now my fear had been replaced by a healthy respect for the sea that would last me as long as I lived. So the swimming was good. It was later, when we'd come out of the water, that I'd been thinking about. Later, when his wet-slick hands had touched me, when I'd responded to his kiss.

I should have stopped him. But it happened so fast, I don't think he planned it. It just happened. But I'd be careful now. I'd remember that, in spite of what had happened, I still didn't like him or trust him. And besides, he was Mary's fellow and David was mine.

And David was right of course. There was something odd about Alan. Certainly he was mixed up in some way with drugs. But still . . . I didn't want to spy on him.

I cleared my throat. "I'd feel . . . shabby . . . spying on him."

"I see." His face looked set and hard.

"Don't be angry, David. Look, if he does something really *heinous* . . . If you think it's important . . ."

"I wouldn't have asked you, if I didn't think it was important."

"All right. I'll keep my eyes open. I'll tell you if I see anything you should know."

I wanted to say something else. I wanted to say, "You're still with the government, aren't you?" but at that moment he said, "There's Euphemia. You didn't tell me she'd be here tonight."

"I didn't know she would be. She didn't say anything."

I started toward her. Then stopped. This was not the Euphemia of the starched calico dress and the clean kerchief and smooth shining face. This Euphemia's face was as dirty as her sweat-stained dress. She wouldn't want me to see her.

She backed up to the truck, braced herself when the big

load of bananas was thrust onto her shoulder, staggered slightly, then started away.

Wordlessly, David and I made our way down the length of the long warehouse until we stood below the ship. No songs here. No laughter. Only grunts of effort as bent bodies struggled up the gangplank. Uhh, uhh, uhh.

We found Samuel when we started back. He was curled up against the wall, hands under his head, his face and his hair streaked with dirt. His mouth hung slightly open, breathing deeply, oblivious to the sounds around him. An older boy sat beside him.

"God, look at him," David said. "He looks like he hasn't slept for a week." He started toward the boys.

"Not yet." I put a restraining hand on his arm. "I want to sketch him." I pulled a crate, sat down, and began to sketch.

David was right. Samuel looked as though he hadn't slept for a very long time. His small face was pinched and strangely wizened. There was a smudge of dirt on his cheek and one on his forehead. A long scratch on his hand. His feet were bare, the soles covered with dirt and dust.

The boy beside him was only slightly older, nine perhaps. He watched while I sketched. Once I looked up, and when I saw the vacant look of fatigue in his eyes I looked away.

"All right," I said finally. "That does it."

David squatted beside the two boys. "Are you Samuel's brother?" he asked.

"I be Ezekiel, sir." There was a quiet dignity in his voice.

"You've had a long night, son."

"Mama say we don't work anymore now. We rest here till she come."

"How soon?"

A shrug. "Two, maybe three hours."

"We could take you home. You've met Mistress

Catherine. I'm sure it would be all right with your mama."

"How's she going to know we be gone?"

"He's right, David," I said behind him.

"You could take Samuel, sir. He's wore out."

"Yes, I think we'll do that, if it's O.K. with you. You tell your mama that Mistress Catherine and Mr. David have him. We'll bring him back in the morning."

He scooped Samuel in his arms. The small head rolled against his shoulder. David gazed down at the child and rubbed the small black head with his, chin.

He shifted Samuel to his shoulder and headed down through the warehouse. I followed, making my way around the end of one of the banana trucks, dodging a fat man pushing a cart, rounding the truck, and almost colliding with a man carrying a hand of bananas over his shoulder. A golden earring glinted in his right ear.

I stared at him. The man from the curio shop in Kingston. The man David had been trying to choke. What in hell was he doing here toting bananas and wearing a ragged pair of cut-offs and a torn, dirty shirt?

"Hey, pretty lady," he said, winking at me. "You looking to find some action? I'll be through here in an hour or two, and if I ain't all tuckered out I'll give you all the action you'll want."

"Stick a banana up your nose, man," I snapped, whipping past him.

And when we were in the cab I told David. "I've just seen that man—the Jamaican from Kingston. What's his name? Franklin? He was loading bananas."

He glanced at me sharply. "You're mistaken, Catherine. It couldn't have been Franklin. There are hundreds of black men in that warehouse. You only caught a glimpse of Franklin. You wouldn't know him if you saw him."

"It was him," I insisted. "I know it was. He offered me a little action later."

"Yeah? What did you tell him?"

"David?"

"O.K., O.K., I'm kidding. Let's drop it. But I'll tell you again—that wasn't Franklin you saw."

I was suddenly furious. He was treating me like a not-very-bright child and I resented it. "Listen . . ." I started to say—when Samuel stirred.

"Mr. David?"

"It's me, kid. You're going to sleep in the hotel tonight. That all right with you?"

"With the two big beds and two big pillows and . . ."

"That was fast," I whispered, forgetting my anger. "He's already gone back to sleep."

"Just so he remembers what I said, so he doesn't wake up scared in the morning. All right if I have the cab take us to the hotel first?"

"Of course. Maybe you'd better get him cleaned up before you put him to bed. If you want some help, I can . . ."

"To hell with the nice clean bed!"

I felt just the least little bit rejected. I wanted to be part of them. I wanted, I think, to feel part of a family, David, Samuel and me. Family.

The taxi let me off at the edge of the road leading down to the beach house. The night was warm, and the air was filled with the sweet smell of jasmine. Only the sounds of the waves and the faint throbbing of crickets broke the stillness. The house stood as quiet as a shadow at the rise of the dune. I wondered if Mary and the others had returned.

I lingered a while, savoring the fresh, clean smells. I wasn't angry now, but I wondered why David had been so adamant in insisting that the man I'd seen wasn't Franklin.

Of *course* it was Franklin!

I opened the top buttons of my blouse and felt the sea air cool me. I wished David had let me go with him. I wished I had suggested we bring Samuel back here and put him to bed. If I had, he'd be here with me now, here on the beach. I smiled, remembering how we'd joked that first night back from Kingston about love among the sand dunes. And suddenly that's exactly what I wanted. Now. I wanted him to pull me down on the sand and make good crazy love to me. And after the good crazy love we could swim naked in the sea.

"Well, hell!" I said aloud. I stretched and yawned and succeeded in laughing at myself. "What you need, my girl, is food. A good, hearty, roast beef sandwich and a long, tall gin and tonic to cool you down."

As I started up the driveway, I slipped out of my shoes so that I could feel the sand with my toes, smiling to myself at my sudden attack of horniness. Maybe it was the sea air.

I was still smiling when I pushed the kitchen door. For a moment the smile stayed frozen on my face. It seemed as though every other part of me was frozen and stilled as I looked into Whitey Koebler's flat, gray eyes.

From across the room I heard an indrawn breath and a coffee cup being set down. My eyes shifted, saw Alan. "I wanted a sandwich," I said, knowing my voice was an octave too high. "There was roast beef . . ."

"Well, well, well," Whitey said softly. "And who do we have here? None other than pussycat Catherine. I heard you were in Jamaica, Catsy-baby. I been hoping I'd run into you."

A white hand reached out and grasped my chin. "You glad to see me? You come runnin' in here just to see me?" His hand moved up to caress my cheek. "Whatcha doing here, pretty Catsy? I thought you were in Kingston."

I jerked away from him. "Take your hands off me," I said."

He laughed. He let me go and turned to Alan. "I thought I saw her in Kingston, but I wasn't sure. I only got a glimpse. Franklin and Dave and I are talking. Dave's mad because Franklin made a crack about his kid. He grabs Franklin by the neck. I'm trying to pry them apart, when all of a sudden I look up and I see a dame standing at the door. She looks exactly like the dame we met at Mary's that Sunday. It strikes me as a very peculiar coincidence that I seen her there and now I see her here."

"And that's exactly what it is," Alan said. "A coincidence."

"Yeah. Sure." The flat, gray eyes looked at Alan, and then at me. I suddenly knew that if I had cried, or pleaded, his face would not have changed. I thought of the girl whose breasts he had cut. "A pretty little thing," David had said. Had she cried? Had she pleaded?

Suddenly Alan chuckled. "Whitey, my man, do you think you're the only reason I came to Jamaica?"

"Whatdaya mean?"

"Take a look at her. What do you think I mean?"

"You trying to tell me you two got something going?" He shook his head. "You haven't known her any longer than I have, pal."

"We had a week to get acquainted before she left for Jamaica. We set it up that she'd agree to do Mary's book and that I'd come later with Mary. A perfect setup."

"Don't shit me, Alan. I seen the way Mary looked at you that night in New York. She had you tabbed as her own special property."

Alan grinned at him. "So I keep her happy. And Cathy and I play our little game on the side."

"Listen, you want a woman, I'll get you a woman. First class stuff. I make a phone call to Miami tomorrow, you got a broad tomorrow night." He looked me up and down. "Tell you the truth, Alan, I kinda got plans for this one."

"Plans?" I shouted. "You've got plans? I wouldn't spit on the best side of you . . . you telephone freak."

Alan reached out and fastened his hand around my wrist. He yanked me roughly to him. "I don't like you to talk to my friends, that way, Cathy. Now behave yourself!" His hand tightened on my wrist.

Whitey's eyes were watchful. "You think she's going to do what you tell her to do? About everything?"

"She'd better."

"She know Dave?"

I could hear the purr of the refrigerator motor. I felt Alan's fingers jerk against my wrist.

"As a matter of fact she does. Ocho Rios is a small place. Mary met him on the beach a couple of days ago. He's been hanging around ever since."

"And Catsy wasn't in Kingston with him?"

"She didn't even know him then. She took the maid's boy into Kingston to see a doctor. Relax, will you? I'll take care of Cathy."

"I don't like it."

"All right, all right! You get too unhappy about her and I'll ship her back to New York. But, damn it, Whitey, I was trying to combine a little pleasure with business." He let go of my wrist and slapped my bottom. "And believe me, Cathy is pure pleasure."

Whitey looked at him through eyes narrowed to slits. Finally he shrugged. "O.K. she's yours. So long as you keep her under control. If you don't, back she goes."

"Agreed." And to me. "You still want that sandwich?"

I shook my head, unable to speak.

"I'll walk you to your room."

"Just a minute," Whitey said. His eyes bored into mine. When he spoke, his voice was as cold as death. "One slip," he said. "You make one little slip, and you're mine. You'll never see New York again. I don't give a shit what Alan says, you do something I don't like, you show up once more where you shouldn't be, and I'm gonna hurt you real bad."

"That's enough!" Alan's voice was sharp. He turned me away from Whitey and pushed me through the door.

We didn't speak as we went down the long hall to my bedroom, his hand still holding my arm. He took me into the room and closed the door. He leaned against it and said, "All right, let's talk about it. Was Kingston a coincidence or did you know David went there to meet Whitey?"

His grip tightened. I winced, and he let me go. "I wish I knew what you were up to, what your involvement with David really is."

"I'm in love with him, that's my involvement. Whitey's just somebody he knew years ago. Somebody who turns his stomach as much as he does mine."

"What was that crack you made about a telephone freak?"

"Your friend Whitey called me that night after Mary's party. Oh, he didn't give his name, but I knew who it was. You've heard of sick phone calls? Well this was a real sicky. He said he, quote, wanted to screw me. He said he wanted to hurt me with his hands and . . ."

"Good Lord!" His face was white.

"And you're involved with him. You let him think that you and I . . ."

"And what do you think would have happened to you if I hadn't told him you were my girl?" He held me hard. His fingers bit into my shoulders. "And from now on, whenever he's around, that's what you're going to be. You're going to smile at me. You're going to say 'Yes, Alan,' and 'No, Alan,' . . ."

"I won't."

"Because, if you don't, I won't be able to protect you."

I swallowed hard. "Why are you mixed up with a man like him?"

"That's none of your business. Whitey and I are working on a business deal. It involves a lot of money. We have to be careful. You've got to promise me you won't say anything to David about seeing Whitey here tonight."

"I . . ." I thought of Whitey waiting in the kitchen. I remembered his words and the coldness of his hand on my face. If I didn't do what Alan asked, would he take me back to the kitchen. Back to Whitey?

"I hate you," I said.

"Promise me you won't say anything to David."

"I promise." My voice was a hiss.

"Or to Mary."

"O.K., O.K."

"And when Whitey's around, you're my girl. Understood?"

"Yes! Now will you go?"

"In a minute. You're my girl, remember. I wouldn't rush off without a kiss—a smudge of lipstick."

"Don't you . . ."

"Only to make our story better. I won't like it any better than you will."

Before I could move away, his arms were around me and his lips were on mine. When I tried to move my face, his hand clamped the back of my head, forcing me to be still while his lips moved against mine.

The kiss was as deliberate and as mean as a slap in the face.

81

When he let me go, he said, quite matter-of-factly, "That ought to do it."

"You bastard," I said softly.

"I'm glad we understand each other." The mocking grin was back. "Sleep well, Cathy, my love. Sleep well and dream of me. I'll see you in the morning."

CHAPTER NINE

The next few days passed in a slow agony of fear. No matter how I tried to avoid Alan, he seemed always to be near. If I rose early to have breakfast at seven, he would be sitting at the table when I came out on the terrace. If I stayed in my room until ten, certain that I would miss him, he would appear before I raised the coffee cup to my lips. Sometimes we were alone, sometimes the others were there. But it was Alan I saw, only Alan, with his mocking grin and strange, green eyes that followed my every move.

Even Mary noticed. "What is it with you and Alan?" she asked me one morning. "What's the strange fascination he seems to have for you?"

"Fascination!" I gave an unlady-like snort. "Malevolence is more like it."

"Really, darling, I can't understand you. You and Alan have been spitting bricks at each other ever since you met. Why?"

I wanted to tell her why, but I couldn't. Instead, I shrugged and said, "Who knows? Bad chemistry perhaps. Once in a while you meet someone who rubs you the wrong way." And wanting to put her off, I added, "Anyway, you like him enough for both of us."

She got up abruptly, went to the bar, and splashed a fair amount of vodka in a glass over ice. She was drinking far too much lately, and her small face had taken on a pinched, taut look.

When she came back with her drink, I said, "What is it, Mary? What's troubling you?"

"Alan. I think he's shacking up with somebody in town. A chocolate-flavored gal, maybe. Somebody with a fresh young face." She slammed her drink down on the table. "Damn! This has been a rotten vacation. I asked Mark and the girls along just to keep up appearances. Well, I needn't have bothered. I'm as pure now as I was the day I arrived."

"You mean Alan hasn't . . ."

"Darling, he hasn't touched me. I'm beginning to feel like a horny Typhoid Mary."

I smiled to myself. I remembered the other night. She wasn't the only one who felt that way.

"I really like him, Catherine. And from the way he acted in New York I rather thought he liked me. But now . . ." She shrugged.

"I was a little surprised that you invited him here."

"I didn't exactly invite him, darling. I mean I did, and I didn't. A week after you left New York he phoned and said he had a cold he couldn't shake, and wasn't the weather rotten, and wouldn't it be wonderful to be lying on a beach in Jamaica."

"And so you . . ." I waited for her to go on.

"I said, 'Look, darling, I've been thinking about going, so if you can get away we'll go together.' Then I rounded up Laura and Kitty and Mark to make it a house party type of thing."

"When you asked him if he could get away, what did he say?"

"He said yes, obviously. Why?"

"What about his job? What does he do? Do you know anything about him? Where he comes from or what he does?"

"Of course not. But what do you know about David? Did you ask him for a dossier before you fell into his arms?"

I felt my face grow hot. "No, but . . ."

"No buts. Most of us take our men at face value and hope for the best."

"Alan's different."

"Different from whom? David? Don't be silly. The only difference between them is age. David's older, you're younger. Alan's younger, I'm older. That's your difference."

"David's not into drugs."

"Well, neither is Alan."

"Oh, Mary!"

"Well, he's not. Have you ever seen him take anything? Have you ever seen him even the least little bit high?"

"I didn't necessarily mean he *takes* drugs. That first night, when we had dinner here on the terrace, you told him to go in and get some grass. Mark asked him what else he had, and he said, name it and he'd check the larder. *That's* being into drugs, Mary."

"Darling, when we arrived I sent him into town to pick it up. He was a messenger boy. He wouldn't have known where to buy it, if I hadn't told him. And, for heaven's sake, don't look at me like that. Don't get all excited because I smoke a little grass or sniff a little coke." She smiled. "Coke is the champagne of drugs. Half my friends use it. Hostesses pass it around in place of after-dinner mints. It's no big, scary thing."

"It *is* a big, scary thing," I insisted. "It's illegal. Too much of it can be addictive, and besides . . ."

"Darling, a lot of perfectly nice people use something once in a while."

"Do perfectly nice people get as spaced out as you were

the other night? When I came back from the beach, you were carrying on a lovely conversation with the palm trees."

She giggled. "Catherine, don't exaggerate."

"And it wasn't from smoking grass. I think Alan gave you something stronger. I don't know about drugs, and I don't know what he gave you but, whatever it was, it was terrible."

"It wasn't terrible at all. It was lovely."

I was saying too much, but I couldn't help it. I wanted to tell her about the other night. I wanted to tell her what Alan really was. How dangerous he was. And I wanted to send her back to New York where she would be away from him. Where she'd be safe.

And if I did tell her? Would she believe me? I didn't think so. She wouldn't listen to me when I tried to warn her about marijuana and coke.

I suddenly felt helpless. It was as though she'd placed a thin sheet of glass between us. I was on one side, trying to talk to her, and she was on the other side, patting her smooth black hair and smiling at me as though she didn't hear a word I said. And I wanted to break that thin sheet of glass and shout at her until she heard me. Because I cared what happened to her.

She was more than a friend. She was my almost sister. I'd known her ever since I could remember. I had gone to school with her younger sister, Liz.

When my father married Isabel, it seemed as though my whole life changed. At first, when she and dad were dating, she tried to pretend she liked me. But after the first three months of her marriage she didn't bother pretending. She simply did not want me in her sight. She stayed in bed until I left for school. And after school I went to Mary and Liz's.

Mary's mother was sensitive to my unhappiness. As the years went by, I began to spend more time in their home than in my own. Mary became as much of an older sister to me as she was to Liz. She drove us to Girl Scout meetings, to movies, and to parties for all of my growing years. She moved to New York while I was still in high school. By the time I finished art school, she had already established herself as a writer.

We lost touch for a while, but later, when I decided to try New York, Liz wrote Mary to say I was coming. When I arrived at the East Side Airlines Terminal she was waiting for me. She took me to her apartment, and I stayed there until I found a place of my own. She got me my first job in New York. Later, when I was ready, she insisted I illustrate her children's books.

I pulled my chair closer and took her hand. I said, "You don't know what might have happened that night. You could have done anything. You could have decided to go talk to the sea. Drugs frighten me. That's why I wish . . ."

She broke in. "Dear, naive Catherine. You're still so wide-eyed and believing. I'd hate anything or anybody who changed that in you. I'd hate David if he changed you."

"He won't change me. But let's talk about you. You and Alan."

I should have told her then. I should have told her about Alan and Whitey. About how Alan threatened me—made me promise not to tell her or David. Instead I frowned at her and said, "How could you have let him give you that awful drug?"

"But he didn't give it to me, darling." She tapped my chin with a long, thin, perfectly manicured finger. "David did."

I stared at her. I pushed her hand away. How could she? "You're lying," I said. "You're lying, and I hate you for it."

Yes, that's what I said. To Mary. My almost sister. And

that's what I have to live with now.

And that night, when I had dinner with David, I told him what she had said.

He laughed. Then he shook his head and said, "You're making such a big thing out of it. You're so naive that you're not to be believed. I'd have told you right away what happened, but you'd have blown your stack. It's no big deal. Mary was mad at Alan. She was nervous and tired from the trip. She said she wanted to get a good night's sleep, but she knew she was too up-tight to rest. She asked me if I had anything. I had some sleeping pills, and I gave her two of them." He shrugged. "Maybe she'd taken something else earlier. They hit her fast and she got a little groggy."

"A little groggy!" I stared at him, unable to believe what he was saying.

"Come on, Catherine. People take sleeping pills and tranquilizers every day of their lives. What's the big deal?"

This was the second time I'd heard this kind of philosophy today. Was I the one who was out of step? "What about you?" I asked. "Are sleeping pills your kick?"

"I take one occasionally. Working for the government was a tough job. The hours were rugged. I saw a lot of things and did a lot of things I wish to hell I hadn't. There are things I'd like to forget." He chewed his lip. "And these last few years, since Davey's been gone . . . Jesus! I close my eyes at night and I can see him pacing a two-by-four cell. Hungry, dirty, sick, maybe crying out in terror or anguish. Wondering why nobody's doing anything to get him out."

He let his breath out slowly. "And I go nuts. I want to smash something. I want to break walls down. I want to do whatever I have to, to get him out."

His hands closed around mine. "And finally, my love, I take a sleeping pill."

I was silent for a moment while I thought about what he'd said. And what I would say to him. Finally I said, "I'm sorry. It must be agony for you."

"And I'm sorry, hon. I shouldn't have given Mary the pills. I'm sorry I didn't tell you."

"It's all right, David. Let's forget it. But I wish . . ."

"What?"

"I'm fond of Mary, you know that. She's been like a sister to me. But I don't understand her sometimes. I wish you and I were still alone—like we were before we went to Kingston. I wish Mary and her friends had stayed in New York."

"Maybe you ought to leave Jamaica, Catherine."

"Let's both leave. We could go to one of the other islands, or . . ."

"Together?" He grinned. "Tsk, tsk, Mistress Catherine. Would'st live in sin with me?"

He chuckled me under the chin. Which was not exactly the type of answer I had hoped for. And then he said, "You go on back to New York, and I'll meet you there as soon as I can."

"Why can't you leave now?"

"I've got some unfinished business I've got to take care of."

"You're still with the government, aren't you? You're on a case, and it's got something to do with that . . . that man. That horrible son-of-a-bitch of a man."

"Catherine! What in the hell are you talking about? I told you I was finished with that kind of work. I told you I just happened to run into Whitey in Kingston."

"He's here. Herein Ocho Rios." I couldn't help it. I'd blurted the words out before I thought.

David's face tightened. "Where did you see him?"

I cleared my throat. I took a sip of my Planters Punch. "In Town."

"The . . . the library."

"Did he see you?"

"I don't think so." My lies were beginning to stick in my throat. I took another sip of my drink.

"Was anybody with him?"

God, how I wanted to tell him about Alan and Whitey. But I was afraid, so afraid. I said, "No, he was alone. Did you . . . did you know he was here?"

He hesitated. "Yes. He phoned me this morning."

"Why?"

"Why not? I used to know him, that's all. Now don't be a nosey broad. And pay attention. The show's about to start."

"But . . ."

He covered my hand with his. "Don't worry about this, Catherine. It doesn't concern you."

We were outside on the patio. The tables were dimly lighted by candles. I could see his face, but not his eyes. Then, suddenly, the patio became alive with light, and in that light David's eyes looked strange and cold.

I pulled my hand away. I looked toward the bandstand as gleaming black bodies exploded into the night, torches held high over their heads, gyrating to the rhythm of the drums.

I opened the sketch pad. My hand moved swiftly as I tried to capture on paper the fine dark bodies as they step-stepped to a limbo bar, chanting, swaying, and one by one, flexed and quivered their bodies under the bar. Lower and still lower the shining bodies bent and wriggled. Finally the slimmest, prettiest Jamaican girl I'd ever seen, wearing the tiniest leopard bikini I'd ever seen, approached the bar. Her sweat-wet body gleamed in the light of the torches as she bent back, back, back to an impossible angle. The muscles on her legs turned to hard golf-ball knots as, step by careful step, to the pulse beat of the drums, she slithered under the bar.

"Hey, hey, hey," the master of ceremonies said into the microphone. "How about that? And now, ladies and gentlemen, from the wild to the wild. Here for the first time, all the way from Trinidad, Matthew Monk and his Marionettes."

A tall black man came onto the stage amid a smattering of applause. He bowed to the audience, opened the large box he was carrying, and went into his act.

He was good, so good that in a moment I was caught up in the childhood magic of the puppets. He did a funny Jamaican version of Snow White and the Seven Dwarfs, which he called Black Belinda and the Seven Duppies. "Duppies," he said in an aside to the audience, "in case you tourist folks don't know, are ghosts that walk in the night and scare everybody to death."

After he put away Black Belinda he pulled a clown out of the box, a funny-looking clown dressed in a red and white polka-dot suit with a red and white polka-dot ruffle around the neck. He wore a red and white hat with a black tassel on top. His eyes were droopy sad and his nose was a bright red ball.

The man handled the clown so skillfully that in a moment it seemed to be a living, breathing, dancing child. At one point the clown reached into the box, fished and flopped around until he found a balloon, a yellow balloon, and then he handed it to the man to blow up. The man blew and blew until the yellow balloon was very large, and then he gave it to the clown. And, like a small boy who was just given a marvelous toy, the clown began to dance. The man smiled a strange, smirky smile. Then he lit a cigarette, puffed until it glowed, and touched it to the balloon.

"Son-of-a-bitch," David whispered.

The little clown began to cry. His small shoulders heaved up and down with his sobs. He struck at the man with small fists and then clung to his legs.

Suddenly, ridiculously, my eyes filled.

The man softened. He patted the clown, found another yellow balloon, blew it up, and handed it to him. The clown dried his eyes and hugged the man's leg. Then he began to dance in a floppy, graceful motion, holding aloft the yellow balloon.

And I was filled with such a hunger, such a yearning, that for a moment it was a physical pain. I felt as I had the other night when David took Samuel back to his hotel, when I had wanted to be a part of them. Part of a family. I'd been on the outside looking in for such a long time, since my mother died perhaps. And I didn't want to be outside. I wanted something of my own. I wanted a baby. I wanted a family.

"That was a hell of an act," he said.

"Yes."

"Hey, you're crying." His hand covered mine.

"David . . ." I tried to swallow the words. I tried, but they tumbled out. "I want a baby," I said. "I want your baby. I want a family."

He took his hand away from mine. His face looked as cold and as strange as it had a few minutes before.

"I didn't mean . . ."

The look on his face stopped my words. When he spoke, his words were spaced and hard. "Davey is the only kid I ever wanted. I was twenty-two when he was born. I'm forty-four now. I will never father another child. I love you. I love being with you. But just you. I don't want another kid. I want Davey. I want my life back the way it was before he went away."

"I hope you get Davey back. But your life—nobody's life—can ever be exactly the same as it once was. But we have to live every day of it. You can't cling to your grief forever."

"I can cling to it as long as I goddamn well please!"

"Then I can't help you. Nobody can help you." I got up and crossed the dance floor.

He caught me at the edge of the beach. He put his arms around me and pulled me to him. He said, "Don't leave me. Don't leave me tonight."

I stayed with him that night. Part of that night. I think we both wanted to assuage our words and to recapture the lovely magic of those first few weeks we'd have together. And it was that way, for him.

When at last he slept by my side, I lay for a long time, thought a lot of thoughts. I thought that perhaps he would marry me. In time. And I thought I could make him happy. For a while. But something was missing. Would I ever find that part of David that he'd hidden away inside himself since Davey had been listed as missing? And what kind of a man could he be without it?

I gathered my clothes and went into the bathroom to dress. I felt a tired, unexplainable sadness. I looked into the mirror and I thought, What now, Catherine-with-a-C? What now?

CHAPTER TEN

I changed that morning, that early dark morning on the beach. The sea was calm, as the first faint traces of dawn pinked the sky. So calm that I could almost forget what it had been like only a few days before. I remembered my fear. I remembered the seaweed and the silvery fish. And I hugged my knees, trying not to be afraid.

I'm afraid of a lot of things, and because I am, I try to pretend that certain things do not exist. Like the pregnant woman who thinks if she pretends she's not, her pregnancy will go away, I close my mind to ugliness. For me there are no muggers or rapists or drug dealers. The policeman on the corner is there only to say good morning or to bum an apple of the fruit man.

Yesterday both Mary and David had said I was naive. They were wrong. I'm not naive—I'm a coward. That's why I turn my back on things I'd rather not see.

But how could I turn my back on David? He seemed—and yes, he *was*—a man of great warmth and kindness. A man with a capacity for love. I thought of the way he had been with Samuel when we were in Kingston. I remembered with what gentleness he had wiped the rain from the boy and had dressed him. But I also remembered the blind rage that had been on his face when he gripped Franklin, the Jamaican, by the throat. What had he to do with Franklin? Or with Whitey?

And why had he given Mary sleeping pills?

Finally I climbed the dune to the quiet house and went silently along the terrace to the unlocked French doors of my room.

Bruce was curled up in the middle of my bed, blinking at the sudden light, looking sour and irascible.

"Hi, you miserable cat," I said, and leaned over to scratch him. He yawned and stretched and permitted himself a soft rumble of a purr.

"You're getting mellow in your old age, boy. Maybe it's Moses. Maybe he's making a changed cat out of you." And in a sudden fit of need, I said, "I wish you could talk. I'm so mixed up. I need so badly to talk to somebody."

His only answer was a slow blink of his green eyes.

But after I was in bed, he left his usual place by my hip and came up to sleep warm and comforting against my arm.

Euphemia woke me at noon. When she came in, carrying a tray of fresh fruit, hot tea, and toast, she said, "I be worried that you be sick, Mistress."

"Not sick. Just tired. I sat out on the beach until dawn."

"You shouldn't do that!" She looked shocked. "The duppies be going to catch you."

I sat up in bed and took a sip of tea. "Duppies? I heard that word last night, but I don't know what it means."

"Everybody that live in Jamaica know about the duppies." She lowered her voice. "They be ghosts that wander at night and bring evil."

I made a face. "And you believe in them?"

"I believe. You want me to explain about the duppies?"

I took a bite of toast, and nodded.

"Well, Mistress, every man has two spirits, one from God and one not from God. And when a man die, the good spirit flies up to a tree, and then on to heaven. But the bad spirit stay on earth and be a duppie. It live in the grave of the dead man during the day but, come night, it wander around. If somebody doesn't like somebody, he go to a grave at midnight. He scoop a small hollow in the ground and put in some rice. Then he sprinkle with sugar-water. Then he whisper to the duppie the name of his enemy. And I tell you, Mistress Catherine, it take a good Obeahman to take the shadow off."

"What's an Obeahman? Something like a witch doctor?"

"Voodoo man with strong magic. And it takes strong magic to take the shadow off, if duppie want you. Worse kind of duppie be a Rolling Calf. If he catch you and give you one lick, you dead!"

"Euphemia! You're scaring me to death."

"Better to be scared than catched by a duppie." She frowned at the open doors of my bedroom. "If you want to leave these doors open all night, least you can do is put a splash of blue paint to keep the duppies out. Because duppies be scared of blue. You don't want a duppie to come in some night and carry you off."

I laughed nervously. But I shivered in spite of myself. Duppies indeed! But what wonderful stories and folklore Euphemia must know. And what an exciting island Jamaica was. Misted mountains, lush, fern-filled valleys, and white sand beaches. And the people—wonderful people like Euphemia. They'd had such a hard history, harder even than the black man in the United States.

They'd been brought from Africa too, of course, but the work they did on the islands was harder, the masters more brutal. There were more than a few Annie Palmer's—the beautiful English woman who was the mistress of Rose Hall. When Annie grew tired of her husband, she poisoned him. She took lover after lover from among her white overseers and her slaves. She'd lived in Haiti for years and was a practitioner of voodoo. She had mysterious and frightening ways of destroying men who had ceased to interest her. She was a sadistic woman who often beat her slave-lovers to death. She buried them in her wide front yard and now, when the palm trees rustle in the wind, the people say the ghosts of Annie's lovers are moaning in the night.

Some of the slave owners cut arms or legs off slaves who tried to escape. No wonder so many of the blacks had turned to voodoo. I wondered how many white plantation owners had felt the lick of a Rolling Calf.

Mary had a few books about the island that I'd already read. Soon I really would go to the library in Ocho Rios to see what I could find. For a long time I'd wanted to do a book of my own. Why not a book on Jamaica? I'd almost finished my sketches for *Island Boy*, perhaps now was the time to do something of my own.

I had a good collection of sketches: of Euphemia and her children, the sellers at Victoria Market in Kingston, the limbo dancers, and the banana loaders. I'd get more. I'd sketch the shopkeepers and the town people. I'd go back up into the mountains and sketch the people there. Perhaps Euphemia would help me, tell me more of her stories. Maybe she'd even take me to an Obeahman.

After I showered and dressed I went out the French doors onto the terrace. Mary and the others were in the middle of lunch and, although for a moment I longed to escape our encounter, I knew that I must face it. I knew that I mustn't allow harsh words to erase all the good years we had between us.

I went over and stood beside her chair. I leaned down and kissed her cheek and I said, "Good morning. I'm sorry I'm so lazy." I hoped she understood that I meant I was sorry for the way I'd spoken to her yesterday.

When she looked up at me, I saw the blue shadows around her eyes and the sudden look of relief. She put her arm around my waist and said, "You look bright as a new penny. The rest did you good."

Mark pulled a chair out for me. "Care for a drink?"

"No, thanks. I've just finished breakfast."

"Had a late night?" Alan said.

I looked into his strange, green eyes, then looked away. "Yes."

"Where were you?" Kitty inquired.

"David and I had dinner at his hotel. After dinner I came back here, and I sat on the beach."

"Alone?" Mark asked.

I nodded. "Euphemia said I shouldn't have. She warned that the duppies might get me."

Laura sat forward in her chair. "What in the world are duppies?"

"Evil ghosts that wander in the night." To myself I suddenly thought, evil white ghosts with flat, gray eyes.

Mary said, "What is it?"

I tried to laugh. "Nothing. I'm . . . fine. What are the plans for today?"

"We're all going out tonight. We're going to have dinner at the new hotel and then go dancing at the Jumbalaya. Call David, will you, darling, and insist that he come along? I want all of us to be together. All right?"

I said yes, and when I called David he said, fine, he'd meet us at the house. After a moment's hesitation he added, "Why didn't you wake me before you left last night?"

"You were sleeping."

"Was anything wrong? Were you still upset about what we discussed earlier?"

"No, I wasn't upset."

"We'll talk about it. O.K.? And we'll do like you said. We'll leave here soon. Maybe hit one of the other islands. Trinidad or Barbados. And there'll be just you and me."

"And after Trinidad and Barbados?"

There was silence on the other end of the line. Then, "New York or Miami. Anywhere you want to go. Don't be angry, Catherine. Try to understand."

I wasn't angry. I only felt an odd emptiness.

I walked my depression off on the beach that afternoon. Mark and Laura came down to join me. We swam and laughed, and I almost forgot how unhappy I'd been the night before. Later, when I was dressing, I told myself that I was going to have a good time that night, and that I would worry about tomorrow tomorrow.

I wore a blue dress to keep the duppies away.

By the time we finished before-dinner cocktails, with-dinner wine, and after-dinner drinks we were all relaxed and in the mood for fun.

When we arrived at the Jumbalaya it was like walking into a party that has started without you. It seemed as though the noise would peel the bamboo off the walls. Yes, that's what struck me—the noise, bamboo walls, and smoke that hung over the room like an old woman's dirty veil. And people—black, brown, tan, yellow, and white people, all jammed close together on the dance floor.

Laura and Kitty looked rapturous. "Isn't it marvelous?" Kitty said.

We found a table for four and three more chairs, and then all seven of us crowded around and ordered drinks. It was impossible to talk. Like everyone else in the Jumbalaya that night, we shouted across the table at each other. We drank rum drinks and fanned ourselves and laughed at jokes we couldn't quite hear. The musicians wiped their sweating faces and played acid rock, Calypso, and ballads from the forties, while we danced.

The night grew warmer and noisier.

When a male voice said, "Dance, Cathy?" I said, yes, and stood up before I realized it was Alan who had asked me. I would have sat back down, I think, but I glanced around the table and saw that Mary was watching me. There was a look on her face that said, please—for me.

I put my hand in his and let him lead me away. I stiffened when he put his arm around me, knowing that he could feel the stiffness of my back against his hand. Let him know how much I dislike him, I thought. But don't let him know you're afraid of him.

The music was mellower now. By the time *Old Black Magic* sequed into *Jamaica Farewell* I began to relax in the movement and the music.

> Oh island in the sun,
> Willed to me by my father's hand,
> All my days I will sing in praise
> Of your sparkling waters, your shining
> sand.

Couples moved slower now, and it seemed as though all of us were enfolded in the blue haze of smoke that hung over the room. Alan and I danced well together. I remember thinking how strange it was that our bodies fitted so well, while we—the kind of people we were—did not. Finally, I suppose, I didn't think at all.

I don't know who stepped closer. Did I? Did he? But it began to seem as though there was only the music and the feel of his shoulder and the pressure of his hand against my back.

That's all there was, and that's all that mattered. Only feeling and sound and touching. I responded to the pressure of his hand bidding me closer. We were suspended in a cocoon of blue smoke. My hand moved up from his shoulder to feel the silky hairs of his neck. My fingers curved around the side of his jaw to touch his face.

The music stopped, and a voice shattered the night. "That's all for tonight, folks." A roll of drums. "Time to close. Time to close."

Awareness. Of who I was. Of who he was. Awareness and shame.

I pulled away from him. I wanted to say, it wasn't you. It was the night and the drinks and the music. But not you, Alan. Never you.

He had no mocking smile now. No smile at all. Just a serious, rather sad face.

We looked at each other for a long moment. Finally, without a word, he took my arm and led me back to the table.

To David.

To Mary.

To Whitey Koebler.

A wolf-grin was on his face when he said, "Well, well, well, imagine running into you two."

I couldn't speak. Without thinking, I put my hand on Alan's arm for support.

"You remember me, don't you Miss Catherine? We met that rainy Sunday afternoon at Mary's apartment."

Alan's arm circled my waist. He nudged me forward. "Yes," I managed to say, "of course. Of course I remember you."

"I thought maybe you did." His laugh was soft. "I heard you were in Ocho Rios. Been kinda hoping I'd run into you and Mary." His flat gray eyes mocked me, dared me to say anything.

"Isn't it marvelous?" Mary said. "I didn't even know Whitey was in Jamaica. And, would you believe it, he and David know each other. Now we're really going to start having fun." She held Whitey's hand. "Aren't we, darling?"

I suddenly realized she was drunk.

"You know it, dollface," he said.

"Let's go back to the house," she said. "We'll have a couple of nightcaps and . . . and whatever." She giggled.

"You wanna ride with me?"

"What do you think?" She swayed when she stood up and would have fallen, if David hadn't grabbed her arm.

"Mary, maybe you have had enough to drink."

"Maybe *you* have, David darling. But not me." She put her arm through Whitey's. "Lead on," she said.

I felt an awful clutching fear when I saw them drive off. I wanted to shout to David to do something, anything, to get Mary away from Whitey. But when I looked at him, he looked away.

When we got to the house, a black MG was in the driveway. As we went around to the beach side I could see the glow of cigarettes on the terrace. And smell the dry, burning odor of marijuana.

When we came onto the terrace, Mary handed her cigarette to David and said, "Take a nice, deep draw, darling."

"Sure. It's a good night for it." He inhaled, held it, then handed the cigarette back to her.

"Your turn, Laura."

"No thanks. I'm playing golf in the morning. I'm going to bed."

"Then you take it, Catherine."

"Nope," I said, trying to keep it light. "I'll pass too."

"Oh, come on. Don't be a spoil-sport. Your little Miss Innocent act is beginning to wear a bit thin." She forced the cigarette into my hand.

"I don't want it," I snapped. I dropped it and stamped it out.

"That wasn't at all nice of you, Catherine. They're cheaper here than in New York but, after all, grass doesn't grow on trees." She giggled. "Well, of course it doesn't grow on trees."

David took my arm and led me to the edge of the terrace. "You ought to cool it," he said.

"Does that mean you want me to smoke?"

"No, of course not. But a couple of drags wouldn't hurt you, and it would have satisfied Mary. She's loaded. It's easier to keep her happy. I wish you'd calm down, Catherine. You look as though you're ready to do battle."

"I am! And I'm so mad, I could throttle you. Why in the world did you let Whitey join us?"

"I didn't have much choice. I ran into him on my way back from the men's room. We had a drink at the bar, and he came back to the table with me. Mary jumped up and kissed him like a long-lost friend. What in the hell was I supposed to do?" His gaze was level. "I think she was teed off because you and Alan danced for such a long time."

I bit my lip. Had he seen us—me—the awful way I'd acted on the dance floor? "Well . . . the music . . . the songs they played were awfully . . . danceable. And the drinks. You know. All of a sudden I was Ginger Rogers." I attempted to grin.

He raised an eyebrow. "O.K., Ginger. But remember, off the dance floor you're *my* girl."

Good Lord! I suddenly remembered that Whitey thought I was Alan's girl. Now what was I supposed to do?

"David, get rid of Whitey, please. Take him back to the hotel with you. Mary's had too much to drink, and now she's getting high on grass. I don't want him hanging around her."

For the second time that night he refused to meet my eyes. "Mary's a big girl," he said. "She can take care of herself."

"Not with a man like Whitey."

"This is her house, Catherine. If she wants him to leave all she has to do is tell him."

"But she doesn't know what he's like," I insisted. I was angry now, unable to understand why he didn't pick Whitey up by the scruff of his neck and throw him off the terrace. "You know what a frighteningly dangerous man he is. I can't understand why you or Alan . . ."

"Alan? Yes, that's right. He and Alan are friends. Why don't you ask Alan to handle it?"

I turned my back on him. I was angry and disappointed. Mary was my best friend. Didn't he realize my concern for her?

"I'm going back to the hotel," he said. "I'm sorry you're upset. We'll talk about it tomorrow. If Whitey makes you uncomfortable, go to bed."

"Yes, I'll do that." My voice was cold.

As soon as he left I told Mary I was going to bed.

"No you're not." Her lower lip stuck out in a pout. "We're all going to have a drink."

"No more for me," Laura said. "I'm off to bed while I can still walk."

"Me too," Kitty said. "Enough is enough. We'll see you at breakfast, and for heaven's sweet sake, don't let anybody call us before noon."

Mary frowned at their retreating backs. Then she said, "You make the drinks, Whitey. Everything's there in the side-board. Stingers would be nice. Nice, strong, minty stingers."

O.K. I told myself. A couple of sips of the drink, then maybe I can convince her to call it a night.

I wanted to be alone. I needed time to think about me. A strange, mixed up me. I loved David, but I didn't understand him. Last night I'd let him make love to me. Tonight I felt a pretty basic response to a man I didn't even like.

"A penny," that man I didn't like said.

I didn't look at him. "My thoughts aren't worth a penny." I swallowed. "Alan, about tonight . . ."

"Rum does funny things to people."

"Perhaps."

"Anyway, you're supposed to be my girl. Or had you forgotten?"

"How could I forget? 'Be nice or else'?"

"Why don't you get out of here, Cathy? I'll tell Whitey I've decided to send you home. You don't belong here. You're out of your element. You're getting involved in something you don't understand." He put his hand on my arm. I felt his urgency. "Let me phone Kingston in the morning and make a reservation for you. I'll . . ." Suddenly his voice changed. He moved closer and draped his arm around my shoulder. "Maybe we'll get away for a few days. Just the two of us. All this company is cramping my style."

"Are you out of your mind?" I said furiously. I started to pull away when I felt a warning pressure of his hand on my shoulder, holding me so that I couldn't draw back when he bent to kiss me.

"Hey, hey," Whitey said, suddenly behind me. "Look at the lovebirds. You better watch it. I think the other dame," he gestured toward Mary, "is mad as hell. But don't worry." He chuckled. "I'm going to take her mind off her troubles."

"You stay away from her," I said.

"You going to make me, sis?" His glance flicked toward Alan. "I warned you. You keep her in line or I'll do it for you." He leaned so close I could feel his breath on my face.

105

"And I'd enjoy it. Believe me, I'd enjoy it." He handed me a drink. "Now, drink your stinger like a good girl."

My hands were shaking. I raised the glass to my mouth and finished half the drink in one, shakey gulp. I looked for a place to put the glass down, but it slipped from my fingers and crashed to the floor. "Oh," I said, and felt the floor tilt.

Alan put out his hand to steady me.

I slapped it away.

"I only want to help you," he said.

"I don't need any help. I'm perfectly all right." But I wasn't. I made my way along the length of the terrace and through the open doors of my bedroom. I kicked off my shoes and tried to unfasten my dress. But I couldn't. I fell across the bed, feeling strange and disoriented. If I could sleep—if I could just close my eyes and drift off . . .

I think I did. For a while. But I dreamed strange, savage dreams. Of graves and duppies. Of a rolling calf with a giant tongue. Of caverns and bats. Of knives. Of white-haired ghosts that walked in the night.

When I shuddered awake, my body was wet with perspiration. But as the dreams began to fade, I smiled and wondered why I had been afraid. Faint pink light came in through the open French doors. The room was a kaleidoscope of color. I was riding a carousel. And the music was a waltz. Dum, dum, da de dum, around and around. My blue dress floated about me. I touched the folds of it, feeling the softness, feeling the color.

The carousel went faster and faster. And then too fast. If I didn't hang on, and I couldn't hang on, and then, and then I was going to slide off, and I . . .

Someone was with me now. Someone who might pull me off the carousel. I said, "Go away. Go away. Don't pull me off. Let me alone. Don't you dare touch me."

"Mistress Catherine. Mistress Catherine."

"I know what you want. You want to pull me off, and I'm not going to let you."

"Oh please, Mistress Catherine."

The carousel horses were running fast now. Breaking away and running around and around and around, their long manes streaking out behind them, their nostrils quivering with excitement. Too fast. Too fast. Now they were sliding. Sliding away.

Two voices. Two faces. One black and one white jumbled into the kaleidoscope of color. White arms held me.

"Go away. Go away. Go away, Dixieland."

"It be the duppies. The duppies come in through those doors and put a spell on her."

"Help me get her clothes off and get her into bed."

My dress being pulled down over my hips.

"Do you know whether or not Mary has a doctor?"

"She have a doctor, Mister Alan, but it take more than a doctor to take this spell off Mistress Catherine. It take Obeahman."

"Maybe so, Euphemia, but I think we'll try a doctor first."

White arms raising me to a sitting position. Reaching around to unfasten my bra.

Sharp, hurting fear. "Don't touch my breasts. Please please please please. I'll do anything you want, only don't cut my breasts." My eyes focusing now. Focusing on the face. On the green eyes. On the green eyes of my enemy.

I tried to squeeze my body into a tight ball. A ball so tight that it would roll, I would roll. Away, away, away from him.

"Cathy, listen to me. Try to think. Did you take anything? Did anyone give you anything?"

The carousel went around and around. Faster and faster.

"Cathy?"

"The duppies gave me the drink." I shut my eyes. "Please don't hurt me."

"I'm going to get a doctor," he said. "Will you stay with her?"

"Yes, sir, Mr. Alan. Won't anything on this island make me leave Mistress Catherine. I stay right here and keep the duppies away from her. But first, I be happy if you close those doors. I knew they be going to get her when I . . ."

The voice trailed off. I reached for her hand and held on tight. And then slowly and gently I slid off the carousel. But Euphemia was there and I held onto her and it was all right after all.

CHAPTER ELEVEN

A doctor with an English accent looked into my eyes and said I'd probably taken Lysergic Acid Diethylamide, and that he would be able to tell more about my condition after a further examination, and would Euphemia please leave the room. She said no, she would not leave the room. The doctor raised bushy gray eyebrows and murmured something about blasted—which he pronounced 'blahsted'—negroes. Then he left. I smiled up at Euphemia, climbed back on the carousel, and sped off into oblivion.

Until voices roused me.

"Why in the hell didn't you call me sooner?"

"I didn't know myself until morning, darling. Until Alan pounded on my door and told me to get a doctor."

"How did he . . . ?"

"Apparently Euphemia came to work by way of the beach. She's got a thing about Catherine leaving her French doors open, so she decided to close them. That damned cat was out on the terrace yowling its head off, and when Euphemia came closer she heard Catherine making strange noises. She went in to her, and then she called Alan, who called me. When I saw her, I knew she was having a bad trip. I told Alan a doctor wasn't necessary but he got absolutely furious and made me call Creighton-Jones and . . ."

"And he said it was L.S.D.?"

"Of course. I didn't need Creighton-Jones to tell me that."

"How did she get hold of it?"

"I haven't the vaguest."

"David?" My mouth felt fuzzy.

"How do you feel?"

"I'm not sure."

"Hungry?"

"Thirsty. May I have some orange juice? Very cold orange juice, with lots of ice." I pushed myself up on my elbows and tried to focus on his face. "What time is it?"

"Ten o'clock," Mary said.

"At night?"

"Yes, darling."

"I lost a day. How . . . ?" I put my hand out. "Euphemia?"

She took my hand. "I be here, Mistress."

"I remember now. You kept me from falling off. But . . . how did I get on the carousel? What happened to me?"

"We'll talk about it tomorrow, Catherine."

"But I want to know. Please."

"Somebody gave you a drug," David said. "L.S.D. You had a very bad trip, but you're all right."

So that's what it feels like, I thought. What a rip-off! Why would anybody risk feeling like that? Could the 'good high' compensate for the kind of terror I'd experienced last night? No way! Drugs were a put-on. The greatest put-on since the Indians accepted a handful of beads for Manhattan. I wondered how many beads they'd take to buy it back. Maybe if everybody in New York got their costume jewelry together . . .

"Catherine!" David was shaking me. His voice was sharp. "Catherine!"

"With enough beads . . ."

"Pay attention, Catherine! I've just told Euphemia she can go. Is that all right with you?"

"Euphemia? Oh yes, lord yes. I'm sorry. You've been here all day, haven't you?" I pressed the hand that I was still holding and smiled at her. "You go home now. I'll be all right."

"It be best I bide here."

"No, you get some rest. I'm O.K."

David put his arm around her shoulders. "Don't worry. I'll stay with Catherine."

"All night." Her voice was firm. "And you be sure those doors be closed."

"All night, I promise. And I'll keep the doors closed.

Mary called for a taxi to take Euphemia home. She brought me a pitcher of orange juice, kissed my cheek, and told me I'd feel better in the morning.

I fought sleep, because when it came the dreams came, deep, bad dreams that I had to claw and push and shudder myself out of. Each time I woke I was reassured by the soft glow of the lamp on David's face. Bruce, unblinking and watchful lay at the foot of the bed.

I held onto my wakefulness as long as I could, fighting to keep my eyes from closing. Then I fell asleep, only to jerk awake again, my body wet with sweat and fear.

I remembered the feel of the cold cloth against my skin when David bathed me. The sound of his voice, the touch of his hands as he calmed me.

Morning came bright with warmth and promise. David got me up, poured hot tea into me, handed me a bathing suit and, when I was dressed, we went down to the beach.

Clear, clean water in the morning. Cool against my legs, chilling around my mid-section, soothing against my face as I cut through the first wave. I felt strength come into my arms and fresh Jamaica air come into my lungs as I reached out, stroking clean and good through the water. I left the bad dreams behind, confident and free again because I knew David was beside me.

We sprawled together on a blanket when we came out of the water. And we lay with our eyes closed to the sun for a long time, without speaking.

Finally I said, "Who do you think gave it to me?"

I felt his arm tense beneath my head. He gently disengaged it and sat up. "Alan."

"No!" I stared at him. "No, it wasn't Alan. Why? Why would he have done such a thing? Because he doesn't like me? That doesn't make sense. It was Whitey. I know damn well it was Whitey."

"I don't think so. Whitey's too cold, too professional. And he's smart enough to know what I'd do if he laid a hand on you." He picked up a seashell and skip-skipped it across the water. "I shouldn't have left the other night, Catherine. I should have stayed until you were in bed—until Whitey'd gone. What happened to you is my fault, and I'm sorry. I've been thinking about it a lot. I think it would be best if you left Jamaica."

"But I don't want to go."

"You said once you wanted us both to leave."

"Will you leave with me?"

"Not now. But . . ."

"No buts, sport. If you stay, I stay." My voice was firm. "Besides, I'm in the middle of something. I've been wanting to tell you about it. I've been reading everything I can about Jamaica, and I've been doing some sketches."

"I thought you were about finished with Mary's book."

"I am. I want to work with Samuel near his home, but two or three days ought to do it. No, this is something else." I knelt on the sand in front of him. "A Jamaica sketchbook."

I wanted him to understand the work I was trying to do.

"I'm trying to capture a picture of a people, David, through the movement of their bodies, the expressions on their faces. The sketches I've already done are good, but I want a lot more. I'd like to go to Port Antonio, and up into the mountains to Mandeville. And I'd give my teeth to get into Cockpit Country. You know about the Maroons?"

"Escaped slaves?"

"That's right. In the early days of slavery the ones who could, the ones who braved the law that said the master could cut off a slave's arms or legs, if he tried to escape, made it up to the Cockpit Country and mixed with the surviving Arawak Indians. The Cockpit Country is so impenetrable that the English soldiers could never find the slaves that hid there. The 'cockpits' are a sort of limestone phenomenon of depressions in the form of upside-down cones. And the whole area apparently is wild with overgrown brush and trees.

"The Maroons used to disguise themselves in green leaves, surround the soldiers that came looking for them, and chop them to pieces. Finally the government gave the Maroons the land in the Cockpit Country so they could stop chasing them. The descendants of the Maroons still live up there, David. They pretty much rule themselves, and they don't like outsiders because they raise ganja. And there are rumors they raise coca."

He sat back on his heels. "Now how in the hell would you know that?"

"Local newspaper," I said, laughing at the startled expression on his face. "Quote: 'The coca bush is grown in Bolivia, Peru, and Jamaica.' Unquote. And cocaine is derived from the coca bush. And, as you undoubtedly know, since you were an agent, cocaine is probably the most abused drug in the United States today. There's been a big increase in it during the last five years, and now it's a multi-million dollar business. Up there, where it's grown, you have to know how to get in and out, and you have to know somebody who'll *let* you in and out. I imagine the coca bush farmers make a lot of money."

"You've gone into this pretty thoroughly," he said. His face looked guarded. "Why all the interest?"

"I'm not interested in the drug part of it, David. All I know is what I've read in the local papers. What I'm interested in is getting up into the Maroon Country to sketch the people."

"I think you'd better forget it, Catherine. Finish Mary's book and head on back to New York. I don't want you running all over the island."

"I could do it, David. I know I could. The railroad skirts a place called Look Behind. You get off at Maggotty Station, and that's only six miles from Accompong, the main Maroon town. I'd have to write for permission, and then somebody would escort me in. I thought maybe Euphemia and I . . ."

"Mother of God, you're out of your fucking mind! If you think for one minute I'd let you go up there . . ."

I stared at him.

He shook his finger at me. "You can't stay out of trouble right here in Ocho Rios. What in the hell do you think would happen to you in Maroon Country? It's none of your goddamn business what the people do up there anyway."

I got to my feet. "Now wait just one damn minute . . ."

"No, *you* wait. You can forget it, because there's no way in the world that I'd let you go up there."

"*Let!?* I'm a free agent, David. There are no rings on my finger or in my nose. I can go anywhere I choose to go."

"Goddamn it . . ." He looked too angry to speak.

"It's what I want to do." My voice was cold.

"What you're *going* to do is get your ass out of Jamaica."

"No, I'm not. Not yet. Look, David . . ." I tried to calm

down. I suddenly understood why he was so angry. "I know why you want me to leave," I said. "You're still working with the government."

He looked startled. "I told you, I quit three years ago."

"You're up to your ears in this, aren't you David? And you're worried about me. You're working on something that concerns Whitey and that Jamaican, Franklin. And maybe Alan. It has something to do with drugs. Like where they come from and how they're shipped out of Jamaica."

His face was set and still.

"So you're going to wait until there's a big shipment—of whatever it is—one that will bring in a hundred thousand dollars or so, and . . ."

"If it's heavy," he interrupted, "if it's cocaine, for instance, a shipment would bring four or five million. Cocaine sells for two thousand dollars an ounce on the street."

I swallowed. "That much?"

"*If!* Yes, it would be that valuable. That's a lot of money, Catherine. A hell of a lot of money. And some men would do almost anything . . ." He looked away from me. "That's why I want you out of here, babe. If anything like that *is* going on, I'd like you out of the way."

"Make you a deal. When you leave, I'll leave."

"Cat, please." His eyes were so suddenly full of trouble. "If you're serious about what you're doing and you don't want to leave the island, then go on over to Port Antonio for a week or two. I'll meet you there."

"When?"

"Later."

I was tempted. But I shook my head. "I'm going to stay here in Ocho Rios," I said. "As long as you're here, this is where I want to be."

We changed the subject then, but even as we talked of

other things, I knew he was still upset. And finally he said, "I've got some work to do. I'm going back to the hotel. I'll call you later."

I watched until he was out of sight, and smiled sadly to myself at his lumbering policeman's walk.

CHAPTER TWELVE

They were on the terrace when I returned to the beach house. And Whitey and Franklin were with them.

Whitey had his arm around Mary's waist. His hand rested with suggested familiarity on her hip.

Franklin was sitting in a lounge chair, his legs stretched out, his white shoes resting on the yellow cushion of a pulled-out chair.

Laura and Kitty and Mark were dressed in traveling clothes. Their suitcases were stacked in one corner of the terrace.

"What in the world . . . ?" I said.

"We're going home," Kitty said. "Today. All three of us."

"But why? You didn't say anything."

"I got a call yesterday," Mark said. "There's a lead part in an Off-Broadway show. They want me for it."

"That's marvelous, Mark, but why do Kitty and Laura have to leave?"

"I'm tired of the golf course," Laura said. "The off-shore wind has ruined some of my best shots. And honestly, Catherine, I just don't like it here any more. Not after what happened to you the other night."

"Imagine," Kitty said, "just imagine somebody putting something in your drink. And the Jumbalaya seemed like such a nice place."

"The Jumbalaya?"

"Whitey said that's the only place you could have gotten the L.S.D."

Franklin made "Tsk, tsk" sounds and said, "You just can't trust *nobody.*"

I glanced at Whitey. He smiled and tilted the glass in his hand as though to say, "Here's looking at you."

"Come with us," Laura said, putting her arm around me. "So much has happened to you here. We'll wait until tomorrow, if you will, Catherine. We only decided to go today because Alan has to go into Kingston and he's driving us."

"I can't, Laura. I still have more work to do on Mary's book, and I'm working on some sketches of my own. I want to see more of the island before I go back to New York."

"If you figuring to travel around de island, you best be careful and stay out of wicked places like the Jumbalaya, Mistress Catherine." Franklin's voice held the loose rhythm of calypso-talk. "That be a shameful, I mean *shameful for true,* thing, somebody puttin' de acid in de drink." He laughed, a high, whinnying laugh. "Look like an ole' stinger sting you for true."

"That's not very funny," Mary said.

"He didn't mean nothin' doll-face," Whitey said, giving her a squeeze. "Just a little joke is all." His gaze swept me. "You feeling better, Catsy, or you still up on Cloud Nine?"

"I'm all right." My voice was cold. I turned my back on him. "I'm going to change," I told Laura. "I'll be back before you leave."

I was glad to get away into the quietness of the house. Away from Whitey's cold, gray stare and Franklin's jeering laugh.

I hesitated outside Alan's door. I was just lifting my hand to knock, when he opened it. "May I come in?" I asked.

"Of course."

He was dressed in dark slacks and a sport shirt. A flight bag was on the floor near the door.

"Kitty said you were driving them into Kingston."

"That's right. I'll be there for a couple of nights. You won't mind being here alone with Mary?"

"No." But I hadn't really thought about it. Yes, I knew I would mind. Especially now that Mary was so caught up with Whitey.

He saw it in my face and said, "Why don't you move over to the hotel while I'm gone?"

"Because Mary wouldn't go, and I won't leave her. Especially now that your friend Whitey is a regular caller. Don't you care anything about her, Alan? Don't you care at all what happens to her? Can't you see the way Whitey's moving in? If you paid more attention to her . . . if you'd . . . well, if you'd . . ."

"If I'd make love to her? Is that what you're trying to say? As a special favor to you? Maybe it's not too late. I'll think about it." His voice was angry.

"I'm sorry. I shouldn't have said anything. It's none of my business. No, I take that back, Alan. It *is* my business. And it will be my fault, if Mary gets into trouble, because I know you and Whitey are up to something. I know how rotten he is, but Mary doesn't. She thinks she's . . . being smart. You haven't exactly knocked yourself out romancing her, so she's going to show you by fooling around with Whitey. When I came in from the beach just now he had his arm around her, and they looked like . . ." I couldn't go on.

"You could tell her what he is, Alan. She'd listen to you. Tell . . ."

I swallowed. My mouth felt dry. My face was suddenly wet with perspiration, and my stomach gave a warning shift.

"Oh, wow," I said weakly.

"Sit down."

I sat down and leaned my head against the bed post. "Do you know anything about L.S.D.?"

"A little."

"I've heard that sometimes people have flashbacks. If that's true . . . if this is . . ."

"It isn't, Cathy. You're still weak from the other night. This will pass in a day or two." He got a cold cloth from the bathroom and wiped my face. "Better now?"

"Yes, thanks." Once again I thought how hard it was to remember I didn't like him. Or trust him.

"Then I want to ask you something about the other night. When Euphemia and I were undressing you . . ."

"Oh my God."

He grinned. "When we were undressing you, you suddenly became terrified about your breasts. You said something like, 'Don't cut my breasts.' That's a pretty spooky thing to say."

I hesitated, then decided to tell him. "David told me that years ago, in Las Vegas, Whitey lived with a girl. A prostitute. He got suspicious of her and came home unexpectedly. He found her with a man and he . . . he cut her breasts. For me, maybe for every woman, that's a horrifying thing."

"God damn it! Why doesn't David do something?"

It was the first time I'd ever heard him swear. "Why don't *you*?" I said. "He's your friend? He and Franklin. Just now, before I came in, Franklin was laughing about my having been 'stung with a stinger,' " I stood up. "It was Whitey, wasn't it? Whitey who put the L.S.D. in my drink?"

"I . . . don't know, Cathy."

I knew he was lying.

"Look, I know you don't like me," he went on, "and I know you're not going to listen to me, but I wish you'd go back to New York."

I was batting a thousand. Everybody wanted me back in New York. Even *I* wanted me back in New York. And I was tired of explaining why I couldn't go—not just yet anyway. Instead, I said, "I don't dislike you *all* the time. How can I? You've pulled me out of the sea and held my hand when I had a not-so-very-nice trip. And besides, nobody who likes Jamaica can be all bad." I put my hand out. "Have a safe trip."

He half smiled and leaned down to kiss my cheek—I think. I turned my head to say, "No, don't." I think. Perhaps it was my sudden movement that made him connect with my lips instead of my cheek. I mean, I *felt* that he was as surprised as I was. And the kiss turned out to be surprised, ferocious, sweet, hard, soft, angry, and tender.

And when he let me go, when he put me away from him, his hands were shaking.

An off-stage superior me observed this and urged the me that was standing there like a dummy to make a fast but dignified exit. I raised my chin, straightened my shoulders, and unclenched my hands. I gave him what I hope was an indignant look, turned, and stumbled over his flight bag.

He reached out to steady me, a laugh tumbling off his lips.

"Don't you dare laugh at me," I said, trying to pull away.

But his hand held me. "You be careful while I'm gone. *And* lock your door. *And* the French doors. Understand?"

I glared at him.

He shook me. "Do you understand?"

"Yes!" I roared.

"If you want me, I'll be at the Sheraton."

"I won't want you."

He raised an eyebrow. "Just in case," he said. "Just in case."

CHAPTER THIRTEEN

The next morning I shifted the easel and the sketch pad to my other hand, glad now that I wasn't carrying my shoes. Euphemia had said, "You don't need shoes, Mistress Catherine. You're going to walk up the beach and back the beach. And you sure don't need shoes to come into my house."

I had explained that I wanted to sketch Samuel in front of his home, and she suggested I come this afternoon. Now I said, "It's awfully warm. Let's cool our feet."

She turned her face into the sun and sniffed the air. "We be going to have an early hurricane season. June through October, that be the season. Most times they don't be coming until September. But when it be hot like this, the hurricanes come sooner."

"When was the last one?"

"1968 or 1969. I don't recollect exactly. But it was a mighty storm. For two days it rain for true. And then the wind came. A terrible wind."

"Was anybody hurt?"

"Lots of folks. My sister who live over in Prickly Pole. Her house blew away. Broke her leg and killed one of her children."

"How awful."

"And some folks over in Port Antonio got washed out to sea. They say the wind blew more than a hundred and twenty-five mile an hour that time. Some of the houses the poor folks have be mighty weak. They be made of almost anything: tin, a few boards, heavy paper, bamboo. And when the big wind come, they be blown away and the folks living in them, they blow away too." She gazed out over the water. "The sea swallow them up."

I looked at the water swirling around my feet. "When it's calm like this, it's hard to imagine it could ever be dangerous."

"Many things be dangerous. It may be I shouldn't say, but those two men, the new friends of Mistress Mary, I think *they* be dangerous." She glanced sideways at me. "That white man, Lord, Lord, Mistress Catherine, he look just like a duppie. That skin that be white like flour, and those stone eyes that look clean through your bones." She rubbed her hands up and down her arms as though suddenly cold.

"You must be speaking to Mistress Mary," she continued. "That black man, that Franklin, you see how he be dressed today? You see those white shoes and those white pants? He look like a rich man. And if he can dress like a rich man today, then how come he be working sometimes down on the dock, toting bananas like the rest of us? I say 'us' because I know you saw me that night."

"Yes, I did, Euphemia. And I'm sorry, I should have said something to you."

"Well, I guess you understand that if a woman has eleven children she be going to spend a lot of her life working. My boys help me and we do just fine. When we all work in the loading shed, we tote as many hands of bananas as we can, and it don't matter which truck they off of. We grab a hand, go to the tally man, and then tote the bananas down to the ship.

"We do—but Franklin don't. He don't often—maybe every fourth or fifth time a ship be in."

"And when he does, he only loads from a certain truck?"

"Yes ma'am. He only load from one."

I felt a shiver of excitement. I knew I'd seen him the night we'd gone to the loading platform. And just why *was* he working? And why only every fourth of fifth ship? The people who were there the night we saw them were there because they had to be. They worked like mules because it was the only way they could feed their families. But Franklin? Euphemia was right. He wore two hundred-dollar suits and hundred-dollar shoes. He didn't *need* to tote bananas!

"I'd like to watch him. I'd like to see for myself what he does. Would you tell me the next time a ship is in? Maybe I could go to work with you."

"Go to work with me?" She laughed. "Lord, Mistress Catherine, you wear an old dress and tie your yellow hair up in a kerchief, and there's still nobody on this island that's going to take you for a Jamaican."

I smiled. "I'm not going to try to be a Jamaican, Euphemia. I'll carry my sketch pad just like I always do. I'll still be the New York artist lady. All right?"

She gave me a doubtful look. "Maybe you better wait until Mr. Alan come back from Kingston."

"Why in the world would I want to wait for him?"

She looked uncomfortable. "Just to ask him if it be all right for you to go."

"I don't have to ask anybody, Euphemia. And I'd certainly never ask Mister Alan." I hesitated. "You like him, don't you?"

"Yes ma'am, I surely do."

"And Mister David? Do you like him?"

"I like him for true, Mistress. He be a fine man—so good with Samuel. Why, he treat that boy like he was his kin."

"Then why wouldn't you say that I should ask *him* instead of Mr. Alan?"

She looked puzzled. "I don't know. I have to ponder on that. It just seem natural to me to say 'Mr. Alan.' I see how he be with you the other night when the duppies put the spell on you and you be mighty sick. You know I like Mistress Mary and I'd never say a word bad about her. But she wasn't herself that night—that morning early when I found you so sick. Seem to me like she was acting *real* strange—not like she usually be. Seemed like I couldn't explain it right to her, about you being sick and needing a doctor. She just kept smiling at me and saying something about everything being just beautiful, and why didn't I stop worrying and see how beautiful everything was. She had a leaf in her hand, a plain green leaf, and she was turning it over and over in her hand and saying, "My, my, isn't this something to see!"

Euphemia shook her head. "So I went and got Mr. Alan, and as soon as I call him he come a runnin'."

Her face was kind. "You were bad off, Mistress. It was all we could do to hold you down on that bed. But Mr. Alan, he hold you good. Strong, so's you can't hurt yourself. But gentle too, like he was holding a baby. Like he *care* what happen to you."

I didn't know what to say. The Alan that Euphemia had just described didn't sound at all like the Alan I knew, the Alan of the mocking smile and the strange, green eyes that could look hard and threatening.

"I know he can be kind—at times," I said. "And I'm grateful to him for what he did for me the other night. And for the time he pulled me out of the sea, too. But there's another side to his character, Euphemia. A side you haven't seen. I think Alan and that white-haired man, Whitey, are mixed up in something bad—something to do with drugs."

"Lord, Misstress Catherine," she said, "don't be saying such things. It be dangerous to talk like that. I wouldn't be surprised at anything that white-haired duppie do, but . . ."

"And while we're talking about duppies, Euphemia, it wasn't the duppies that made me sick. Somebody put something in my drink. I can't prove it, because I didn't see him do it, but I'm sure it was Whitey."

"If it was, then Mr. Alan is no friend of his. And *that's* something I know for true!"

We walked the rest of the way in silence.

Her house was set back from the beach in a settlement of nine or ten houses. The walls of the houses were bamboo. The roofs were made of palm fronds. A white picket fence served to rim the yard and to pen two goats and a scattering of chickens. Ruby red bougainvillaea covered the front of the house. Coconut palms, jacarandas, and breadfruit trees contributed a Gaugin warmth.

Six or seven little boys skittered in and out of the house, wooping in happy shrieks. Moses sat on the bottom step of the porch, holding Bruce in his arms.

"Will you bide with us for dinner? I be fixing pepperpot soup and saltfish. And if you be sure you won't stay here until Mr. Alan come back, then I'll send Samuel over to Mistress Mary's later. He'll stay with you till Mr. Alan come back from Kingston." Her face was set and determined. I could see how she managed to keep eleven active boys in line.

I was sorry that I'd said anything about Alan. I was fond of Euphemia, and now I'd upset her. And one thing I didn't need was a seven-year-old protector. But I smiled and said I couldn't stay for dinner, that I had a date with David and that, honestly, there was no need for Samuel to stay at Mary's."

She put her hands on her hips and said, "*I* be feeling better if he be with you. He's little, but he be a good boy. Something happen or you need something, you send Samuel for me."

I have sense enough to know when I've lost a battle, so I said, thank you very much, set up the easel and went to work.

When I stopped to look at my watch it was after five. I called in to tell Euphemia I was leaving. I looked around for Bruce and found him swatting the petals of a hibiscus. "Time to go home, champ," I said, and bent down to pick him up. And dammit, he hissed at me.

"Hey," I said, "it's me. Remember? The lady who feeds you?"

"He ain't goin'," Moses said. He stood in the doorway, hands on his hips, three feet tall, and ready to do battle.

"Look, honey, you can visit Bruce whenever you want to. And he can visit you. But I'm going to take him home now."

"My cat!" he yelled.

"No dear," I said patiently, "he's *my* cat. Your mama's got enough to do taking care of all you boys. She doesn't need a cat to worry about."

His lower lip wobbled.

"Now, honey . . ."

His mouth turned down at the corners. His face squinched up, and he began to howl—blood-curdling, man-sized howls. Fifty-year-old tears ran out of his two-year-old eyes. Bruce moved in and out of the small legs, his tail a-quiver with emotion. Moses scooped him into his arms.

"Mine," he sobbed.

"Oh, hell," I said. "You probably deserve each other."

I heard a laugh and looked up to see Euphemia standing in the door.

"You've acquired a cat," I said. "Do you mind?"

"Wouldn't do me no good if I did. It don't seem like anybody going to separate those two. You sure it's all right with you? You sure you won't be missing him?"

"I'm glad to get rid of him!"

But I wasn't. I felt just the least bit bereft as I went back up the beach. And mad. That rotten cat hadn't even given me a farewell meow.

CHAPTER FOURTEEN

No one was at the house when I arrived. While I was grateful that Whitey and Franklin were not there, I felt uneasy. I didn't like the idea of stripping down and closing myself in the shower stall.

I went out on the terrace and mixed two gin and tonics, filled them with ice, added a slice of fresh lime, and sat them in the cooler.

I told myself that, thank goodness, Bruce was off my hands. He was a lousy cat and I was damn lucky to be rid of him.

And then I told myself that the stuff leaking out of my eyes was caused by the sea air and I was probably coming down with a cold.

When David arrived he said, "Why are you sniffing?"

I said, "Who's sniffing?" and downed my gin and tonic in stony silence.

After I'd had my shower and dressed I told him about Bruce. "It's the best thing," I said.

"Of course."

"I mean, how in the world can I cart a cat around everywhere I go?"

"You can't."

"Of course not."

"And he's such a damned ornery cat."

"Orneriest cat I ever saw. I'm really glad I'm rid of him."
He patted the top of my head.

I told him about my bodyguard.

"Some bodyguard," he said. "The kid weighs fifty pounds soaking wet, and he sleeps like he's been pole-axed. I can recommend a guy who weighs in at one-eight-five and who, with the slightest encouragement, will stay awake most of the night."

I shook my head. "Sorry, I think the job's been filled. At least for tonight. But I'll let you know if a vacancy turns up."

"I've got to make a phone call."

"Tell her you're all tied up for the night."

"I'm going to tell her my place has been taken by a fifty-pound midget."

We had a good evening. We danced, we laughed, and we held hands and spoke of happy things. Just before we left the hotel, he was paged.

I toyed with my drink, enjoying the night and the music, the music of Jamaica:

> Oh island in the sun,
> Willed to me by my father's hand,
> All my days I will sing in praise
> Of your shining waters,
> Your burning sand.

When he came back, he handed me a brown paper bag. "Present for you, Mistress Catherine," he said. "I don't want you to have to sleep alone tonight."

"You brought me another bottle of champagne?" I laughed.

But I stopped laughing when I opened the bag and pulled out a small replica of the clown we'd seen a few weeks before.

He was dressed in a red and white, polka-dot suit with a red and white, polka-dot ruffle around his neck. He wore the same red and white hat with a black tassel on top. His eyes were droopy sad and his nose was a bright red ball. David had pinned a yellow balloon to his hand.

"Oh, David," I said. "Oh, darling."

"He's got a better disposition than Bruce, and he doesn't shed."

"How did you . . . ?"

"I found the guy with the marionettes."

"Thank you." I leaned forward and kissed him. "He's the nicest present I've ever had. I'll always keep him."

Then, as we had done that first evening, we walked barefoot up the beach. We sat for a long time at the foot of the sand dune. We didn't talk, we just sat very close and listened to the splash of in-shore fish, the splat of the waves, and the gentle rustle of palms moving in the wind. And we kissed with kindness instead of passion.

When at last, hand in hand, we climbed the dune to the house, we found Samuel asleep in one of the chairs. David carried him into my bedroom and put him on the chaise. He didn't stir when I placed a pillow under his head and covered him with a sheet.

At one-thirty we heard a car stop, a door slam, and voices. I felt my body tense. "Listen," I said, "if Whitey's with her, I'll take Samuel and move over to the hotel with you. I won't spend the night in the same house with him."

But she was alone.

"Hi," David called to her. "We're over here. Have a big evening?"

"Big enough, darling. We gambled."

"But there aren't any clubs here, Mary," he said. "Gambling's illegal in Jamaica."

She patted his cheek. "Ah, but your friend Whitey took me to a special place. Between here and St. Ann's Bay. A big beautiful place, with an old-fashioned antebellum look. It was completely deserted, ghostly and beautiful in the moonlight. Tall white columns, long empty porch, creaking shutters. But still regal, still elegant. I could almost see the carriages driving up with ladies in ball gowns and handsome men handing them down to liveried servants." She gave a small shiver of delight.

"We went around to the back, and there in the shadows, were other cars. And when we knocked at the back door, it opened a crack and a man handed us a candle. We slid in and he closed the door and guided us through a part of the house and down some stairs." She laughed. "You wouldn't believe it. The whole, huge cellar has been converted into a gambling casino right out of a Hollywood set. Absolutely fantastic, David. Your friend has marvelous connections."

"He's not exactly my friend, Mary," David said carefully. "I knew him in Vegas years ago. He's an odd sort of a guy and I'm not sure you . . ."

She laughed. "David, I'm a big girl. I can take care of myself. Now, let me fix you a drink."

"No thanks. I'm going to run along." He bent down and kissed my cheek. Then he kissed Mary.

After he left she said, "He's a very nice man."

"Yes he is. Now let's talk about a not-very-nice man.

"Catherine, if you're going to tell me I shouldn't see Whitey . . ."

"That's exactly what I am going to tell you. I think you've taken up with him because you're angry with Alan." I tried to see her face through the darkness of the night. "And maybe with me."

"Why ever for, darling?" Her voice was forced.

132

"I think you might have misinterpreted our dancing together the other night. I think it made you angry, and I don't blame you. I'd had too much to drink. One more rum and I'd have gone into my Sadie Thompson number. But it was the rum, Mary, and I'm sorry. You know I wouldn't deliberately do anything to hurt you."

It was a nice speech. I was a lovely girl. A real winner. I tried not to remember that Alan had kissed me that morning.

"There are other men in Jamaica," I went on. "Gorgeous, living, breathing men. Tourists. Always plenty of those around. English landowners, rich-as-sin Jamaicans. Take your pick. I'm even beginning to think Alan's not so bad." I reached out and took her hands. "He'll be back in a couple of days. I'll go on over to Port Antonio and give you two a chance to be alone. I'll admit I didn't like him at first, but compared to Whitey he's a prize. What I'm trying to say, dear, is that I'd rather see you go out with anybody on this island except Whitey."

"Oh, Catherine . . . a few dates! What's the harm?"

"O.K. I'm going to tell you something. Years ago, when David knew him in Vegas, Whitey was living with a girl. She was a prostitute—an ex-prostitute. He got suspicious of her, and one day he asked somebody to hold down his job, and he went back to their apartment. He found her with another man and he almost killed her." I hesitated. I didn't want to frighten her, but I wanted her to realize what kind of a man she was playing with. I took a deep breath and said, "He cut her breasts, Mary."

I heard her indrawn breath. And then a small forced chuckle. "Darling, for some macabre reason David is trying to frighten you. And you're trying to frighten me. I'm sorry, but I don't believe you."

"Mary, I believed David when he told me. I want you to believe me now."

"I know that Whitey's a little . . . menacing . . . in an attractive sort of way. But that's rather exciting to a woman, don't you think?"

"No, I don't."

"Well I find it exciting." She ruffled her short, smart hair. "A man like Whitey might beat a woman—but mutilate her! No, Catherine, I don't think so. A man would have to be terribly sick to do a thing like that."

"Or terribly vicious."

"But he's not like that, darling. He's been nice to me." She smiled, a slow I've-got-a-secret smile. I felt my stomach turn.

"You've been to bed with him," I said.

"Right on, darling."

"Jesus, Mary."

"And it was nice. Very nice indeed. A little rough, perhaps, and more than a little forceful. But I found it . . . different. I rather liked it. We were here, on the terrace. I got up, I remember, to fix us another drink. He came up behind me and turned me around. He said, 'I want you, doll-face.' And I said something like, 'Behave yourself.' " She chuckled. "And he said, 'Can the shit, Mary. You want me as much as I want you.'

"Not a very romantic approach, was it? Then he yanked me over against him, and I slapped his hands away. He grabbed my wrists with one hand and put his other hand on the top of my dress and ripped. The dress came apart like a piece of paper. And then, before I could do anything or say anything, he pulled me down on the chaise.

"Nobody had ever treated me like that before, Catherine. James Alexander Montgomery always performed as though he were wearing white gloves and black tie. And only on Saturday night after Lawrence Welk. I *earned* this house! Life with James was like living in a bowl of luke-warm oatmeal. I've earned some fun. I thought I was going to have it with Alan, but it didn't turn out that way. Don't begrudge me a small romp with Whitey."

"I don't think he's the type of man you have . . . a small romp with, Mary."

"Whatever it is, darling, I'm enjoying! Now, let's forget it and have a nightcap. Tia Maria over ice?"

When I nodded, she said, "I had a letter from Liz this morning. The new baby is due in December. Four children! I don't know what she's thinking of."

"I do. She always said she wanted a dozen. Jerry's a good husband and a wonderful father. Liz is as contented as a cup-cake."

"And as fat as one! I'm glad you had the good sense not to get married right out of college."

"Ummm. Still, I envy her in a way. She's settled. She knows exactly where she's going and who she's going there with. I'd like to see her. Maybe when we leave here I'll go for a few days. I miss her. I miss the town."

"I do too, I suppose. We had some good times, didn't we?"

"Yes, thanks to you. You spent half your time carting Liz and me wherever we wanted to go. You taught us to dance, how to dress, how to put on makeup. Everything. You made it easier for us, Mary. Liz was your sister, but I was just . . . ."

"You were a sister too, Catherine. You still are. You were a lovely child. There are times when I still feel mother-hennish about you."

"And I feel mother-hennish about *you.*"

"But you mustn't, Catherine. I know I shock you some-times. But I'm not as bad as I pretend to be. I drink a bit too much, I smoke grass, and very occasionally I pop a pill. I even sleep with the wrong men. It's just . . . well, I've been around the track a time or two, darling, and sometimes I get depressed thinking about it. Then I need a lift."

"What happened with the marriages?"

"Who knows? I married Sam for love, Lou for laughs, and James Alexander Montgomery II for money." She raised her glass. "Let's drink to James Alexander Montgomery II. He bought me this house."

I raised my glass. "Here's to him."

We clinked glasses and giggled.

Like girls.

Like young girls.

CHAPTER FIFTEEN

The night was hot and still. I sat in the living room, waiting for midnight, watching Samuel, seventh son of Euphemia, asleep on the sofa. At twelve-thirty I would go to the loading platform to meet Euphemia.

I wished I had a diary. I had one once. I came across it a few years ago and leafing through it, I found it hard to believe I'd been that young. The love of my life at that time was Jerome Simoski, and most of the entries concerned him. On July 2, 1958, he put a bug down my back. On July 6 he chased me with a garter snake. And on August 1 we played post office and he sent me a special delivery letter. I noted that great event with six exclamation points.

Tonight I longed for a diary. My thoughts needed to be put down in an orderly fashion instead of jumbling around inside my head the way they were.

Mary: I vowed I would do everything I could to get her away from Whitey. I had never asked her about her marriages before. If I thought about them, it was with something like amusement. A there-she-goes-again attitude. I hadn't even tried to understand that each failed marriage brought a certain pain and left a certain wound.

David: Why do I feel a small niggle of doubt? Am I afraid that I can never replace the space in his heart that is filled with fear and longing for his missing son? Am I afraid he will never be quite the man I want him to be so long as that space lies empty?

He was born too late, I think. He has the look about him, the look of a man who needs to find new worlds to conquer. He should have stormed up San Juan Hill with Teddy Roosevelt. Or stood on the deck of a ship with Henry Morgan and swashed a buckle or two. But there are no more San Juan Hills or Henry Morgan-type pirates.

Can I reconcile the kind of life I want with the kind of man he is? I've been in New York for three years. But, like millions of other New Yorkers, I'm a transplant. Michigan blood runs in my veins, visions of Michigan housewives romp in my head. I'm Mid-west enough to want a husband who is going to come home to me every evening—a husband I can phone, to ask him to pick up a loaf of rye bread on his way home from the office. I don't think David is a rye-bread type man. Do I change or does he? If you love a man, don't you go where he goes and live the kind of life he wants to live? Yes, of course you do. And I am stuck with it, because if I love David, then I will have to live his kind of life and to hell with the rye bread.

Alan. Better not to think.

I tied my hair back in a kerchief, slipped into sandals, picked up my sketchbook, and left for the loading platform.

Outside, the night was eerie-quiet. The air was heavy with humidity. That afternoon the radio warned that we were in for a blow. Hurricane Gladys, packing winds up to a hundred and thirty-five miles an hour, had hit the Dominican Republic, was moving across Haiti, and veering east. The forecast was indefinite—maybe she'd hit and maybe she wouldn't. I tried to forget what Euphemia had told me about Port Antonio. I wasn't going to worry about a hurricane tonight.

Once again I was amazed at the mass of people running back and forth across the loading platform, the dozens of trucks loaded with bananas, and the incessant hum of so many voices. And the staggering, back-breaking work.

> "Come Missa Tallyman, come tally me banana
> Day dah light, an' me wan' go home
> Six han', seven han', eight han', bunch!
> Day dah light, an' me wan' go home."

I drifted toward a group of tourists, thinking that I would not be so conspicuous if I seemed to be with other people. I found an upended crate, sat down, and began to sketch, keeping an eye out for Euphemia. We had agreed that I would keep myself busy sketching and that, when and if Franklin showed up, she would signal me.

I had not told Mary or David what I was going to do. The three of us had a drink together. Then David and I went out to dinner, and Mary waited for Whitey.

Part of my being here tonight was for her. The sooner Whitey and Franklin were exposed, the sooner I could get Mary away from here and back to New York.

I could not reconcile the fact that she was sleeping with Whitey. "Nobody is all white or all black," someone once said. "There is some good in every living person." O.K. He was clean. His slacks were always neatly pressed, his polo shirts spotless. And he must have worn a new pair of clean white sneakers every day of his life.

But, clean or not, how could Mary let him touch her?

I'd almost told David tonight, but an old-fashioned 'females-do-not-snitch-on-each-other' philosophy kept me silent.

By one o'clock my back ached, and most of the tourists had gone.

It was almost one-thirty before Euphemia motioned to

me. Slowly I drifted in her direction, stopping to make a rapid sketch or two on my way, searching the area she had indicated.

I hesitated when I spotted Franklin. He was bare from the waist up, and his brown body glistened with sweat. He wore a folded red kerchief around his forehead, ragged sandals on his feet.

I watched him for twenty minutes. Euphemia was right. The other workers loaded from whatever truck was handy. Franklin loaded from only one. He'd get a hand of bananas, go to the tally man, hurry down the length of the warehouse to the ship, and return as fast as he could to the same truck.

I began to sketch him, because he was Jamaica too. His mahogany-colored body was tall and muscular. His face was broad, almost handsome. The golden earring in his right ear glinted as he moved.

The driver stood beside his truck. I sketched him too. And the truck. And the bananas. I wasn't sure what I was looking for. Franklin loaded from just this truck. He, and he alone, carried each hand of bananas down to the ship. So they were smuggling something out in the bananas? How did you get something inside a banana?

I felt my skin tingle with excitement. I wished I hadn't come alone. I should have told David what I was doing. He should be the one to see what was going on. Well, O.K., he wasn't here, but I was. I'd watch, and then I'd find David and tell him what I'd seen. He'd do his job and we'd leave Ocho Rios. We'd go to Port Antonio for a pre-honeymoon vacation. We'd get married and somehow we'd work out the Davey problem.

Meantime . . . I signaled Euphemia and she came to stand beside me.

"I want to get a look at one of the hands of bananas," I

said. "Do you suppose you could distract the driver next time Franklin carries a load down to the ship?"

"What are you aiming to do?"

"Steal a hand off the truck and take it some place so I can examine it."

"You just going to walk up to that truck as calm as you please and pick up one of those hands and mosey on out with it?" She laughed. "Ain't no way you can do that. In the first place, a hand be heavy, and you got to know how to handle it. In the second place, you tote a load out of here and everybody going to know it."

"But I've got to get a look at one."

"Then you be talking to the driver." She glanced at my sketchbook. "Show him the sketch you made, tell him how good looking he be. Get him around to the front of the truck and I'll steal you the bananas." She glanced around quickly. "You see that door over to the right side? That lead to another room. Next time Franklin leave with a load, you go right up and start talking to the driver. You keep him looking at you for five, six minutes. And then you go fast as you can for that side door. That's where I'll be."

"It's a good idea but . . ." I hesitated. "I don't like to get you involved in this."

"If you got the determination to do this, then I 'spect I better help you. Now, you go along. And remember, you try to keep him busy for five or six minutes."

I waited until Franklin disappeared into the crowd, and then I ambled over to the driver. "I've been sketching you," I said. "Want to see?"

He looked at me suspiciously, his face a mask of distrust.

I handed the sketch pad to him. "See? I think I've caught you fairly well. Although you're taller than I thought. Look, I'd really like to get this right. Why don't you lean against the side of the truck and I'll try another one. Put your foot up on the bumper. Yes, that's good. And roll your shirt sleeves up a little more. You've got terrific arms."

He smiled self-consciously.

"No, don't smile. I think . . . yes, a more serious look. That's it. Maybe a little frown. Makes you look awfully masculine."

I sketched as I chatted. Then I ripped the page out of the sketch book and handed it to him. "Here you are. How do you like it?"

"Whoeee! You sure be fast, lady. And good. This look like a photograph."

"Don't tell anybody I sketched you, O.K.? If you do, then everybody will want me to do them, and I just do special people."

Euphemia had the bananas now. She was moving fast, heading toward the side door.

"Sure, lady, sure," the truck driver said. He folded the page over once carefully and put it inside the truck. "Thanks a lot."

"You're welcome."

Euphemia had disappeared, and in the distance I could see Franklin making his way back through the mass of people.

"Guess I'll mosey up toward the ship. Maybe sketch the workers going up the gangplank." I started to move away.

"Whoa there," he said.

"What? What is it?"

"I almost forgot." He reached back in the truck and took the sketch out. "You forgot to put your name on it."

I almost yanked it out of his hand. I wrote "C" and stopped. Damn, I couldn't very well sign "Catherine Adams."

Over the driver's shoulder I could see Franklin shoving his

way across the crowded warehouse.

Write anything, I told myself. "C"—what starts with a "C"? My hands were wet. I scrawled "Carry Nation" across the bottom of the sketch and thrust it at him.

"Carry Nation," he read slowly. "That be a mighty pretty name. I surely thank you, Mistress Nation."

"Welcome," I gasped.

Franklin was coming fast. In another moment he would see me. I turned away and made for the side door. An enormously fat woman waddled slowly in front of me. I tried to move around her, but just as I did, she moved ponderously to block my way.

I glanced frantically in Franklin's direction. Fifteen yards, Twelve yards. Coming fast.

In desperation I pushed the fat woman out of the way and sped around her. Then, dodging in and out of the moving loaders and trucks, murmuring "Excuse me's" and "Sorry's" as I ran, I made for the door.

It was dark inside. I stood for a moment, trying to get my bearings. Listening. Wondering if anyone had seen me. If anyone had followed me.

A hand reached out and touched mine. I gasped in terror. "Shhh, Mistress Catherine. It be me, Euphemia. Did anybody see you come in?"

"I don't think so."

She led me down a corridor in the dark, and then she opened another door and we were in a storeroom. A single, naked light bulb hung from the ceiling.

"Was it alright? Was he suspicious?"

"Until I showed him the sketch and told him how masculine he was. It went all right, Euphemia. He didn't suspect anything. Franklin almost saw me. But I'm sure he didn't."

"I got the bananas, but I don't see where anybody going to hide anything."

"Neither do I, but let's give them a look."

I rolled the hand over gingerly, remembering stories of banana spiders. One bite and you were dead. How many times had I heard that when I was a child?

Now it took determination to reach in among the green bananas. I couldn't find anything and I wondered why I'd thought anybody could hide anything here. Still, something had to be valuable enough to make Franklin wear ragged clothes and work like a horse for half the night.

"Damn!" I said finally. "I can't find a thing."

Euphemia hefted the hand slantwise off the crate. "Maybe the stem. I hold it up and you look."

I remember now the feel of the dark, stump-like stem of that hand of bananas, the bottom of the stem smooth to my touch. And the sudden awareness that, it shouldn't be smooth. I felt around it, and then with my fingernails tried to scrape it off. "If only I had something sharp," I muttered.

Euphemia reached into the bosom of her dress and pulled out a sharp folding knife. "We carry these when we work. Sometimes it be necessary to cut a branch that scrape a shoulder."

I opened the knife and gently gouged the edges of the stem with the blade. An inch-round plastic disc came off in my hands. I looked up at Euphemia, feeling my heart thump hard.

I reached my fingers up into the hollowed-out stem and touched cellophane. I pulled out a skinny, three-inch packet of a white powdery substance.

Euphemia gently lowered the bananas to the packing crate.

I held the package out. "There must be one just like this in every hand of bananas Franklin is loading on that ship," I said. "Hundreds of pounds of it."

"What is it?" She looked frightened.

"Cocaine, I think. I'm not sure."

I remembered how much David said a shipment of cocaine was worth. Four or five million dollars. Two thousand an ounce on the street. My God—truckloads of bananas! if each stern held a package like this . . .

"There's so much money involved," I said.

"Is this the thing that grow from the coca bush?"

I nodded.

"That's bad bad stuff. Lot of people been killed because of that coca bush. One time, up in the Cockpit Country, there was a lot of trouble. The police came in and burned all the coca bushes. There were fights; a lot of people were killed. Maybe . . ." she hesitated. "Maybe it be best we leave it here and forget we ever saw it. This be mighty worrysome business."

"I don't like it either, Euphemia. But I have to take it to the police, or to David. He used to work for the government, in this kind of thing. He'll know what to do. I don't want you involved any more than you already are. As soon as we're out of here, you go back to your home. I'll take care of the package." I put it inside the folder with my sketching things.

"We'd best be getting out of here. If other people know there be this kind of business going on, they might have men watching."

"I'm ready. Let's just put the bananas behind these crates. We don't want anybody to discover we've been here. At least for a while."

She turned the light off, took my hand, and led me down the hall. She opened a door, peered out, and then started to guide me out to the alley. Suddenly her breath hissed in her throat and I felt myself being pushed backward into the hall.

She pulled the door closed behind us and we stood in pitch blackness.

"What is it?" I whispered.

"The duppie!" There was terror in her voice.

"The duppie?" I felt my heart lurch. "Whitey?"

"I told you . . . Lord, I told you . . . they creep around in the night. Creep around to do their evil. And I knew the first time I see that man that he be a duppie for true."

I held tight to her arm, and together we waited in the darkness. I could feel sweat trickling down the inside of my arms, staining my dress.

We backed slowly down the hall. Again we stopped and were silent.

The sharp click of heels sounded against stone. And drew closer.

"He be coming!" Her voice was so low I could barely hear her. Her hand clutched at mine in the darkness. I felt myself being pulled backwards farther down the dark hall. She stopped, searching with her hands, trying to find a doorknob.

The door to the alley opened, casting a dim light down the length of the hall. We flattened ourselves against the wall, I could hear the soft brush of her hand, searching, searching. I heard the soft click as she found it, opened a door, and pulled me inside.

I held my breath. In that one instant of light I had seen the gleam of his white hair. And now, as we listened to his approaching footsteps, I thought of his words the night I found him and Alan together. "You show up once more where you shouldn't be, and I'm gonna hurt you real bad."

What would he do? To Euphemia? To me?

The steps were outside the door. Beyond. And, at last, we heard the sound of a door swinging shut.

"Let me look," Euphemia whispered. She opened the door a crack. "You stay here." She stepped out into the hall.

She was gone only a moment or two—but they were long moments. I still remember standing there in the dark, listening to the sound of my heart thumping. Then the door opened a crack and she said, "It's alright . . ."

When we were safely out on the street, she said, "He almost caught us." Her face looked pinched and frightened.

"It's my fault," I said. "I shouldn't have involved you. It has nothing to do with you."

"No way in this world I would let you do this by yourself. You don't . . ." She stopped and glanced around.

The night was strangely still. Then we heard the sound of hammers. "Look at that," she said, pointing to the row of shops. "They know that hurricane going to come for true."

Owners stood outside their shops on stepladders, chairs, and boxes, hammering shutters and boards into place. The ones who didn't have shutters or boards criss-crossed wide strips of brown tape across the plate glass.

The hurricane! I'd almost forgotten.

"It's going to be here by morning," Euphemia said.

"But the radio said we'd maybe get the edge of it. It's supposed to go east of us. It plowed through Haiti this morning."

She sniffed the air. "It won't be going east. It be coming here, and soon. Maybe an hour, maybe two. But soon it be starting. By early morning it be blowing for true. You best be settling down somewhere."

I nibbled my bottom lip. "If you really think it's going to hit us, I'll go back to the beach house and get Mary and Samuel. I don't want them to stay alone. We'll go to David's hotel. I'd like to give him this package just as soon as I can. But if you want to, I'll take Samuel to you before I go to the hotel."

"He be safe with you. I know after that day you pull those

sea urchins out of his feet into your own hands that, no matter what, you'd watch over Samuel like he was your own. And he be tickled to stay in the hotel again."

"And what about you!" I remembered the bamboo walls and the palm roof of her house. "Will you and the other children be all right? Look, maybe you'd better come to the hotel with us. We'll get a taxi and go to your place first. You get the children. We'll pick up Mary and Samuel and we'll all go to the hotel."

When we found a taxi and settled in, Euphemia leaned close to me and whispered, "As soon as you give that package to Mr. David you tell him to go to the police and take you with him. If Franklin find out what we done, he going to be one mad black man."

She settle back into the taxi and in a normal voice said, "I surely appreciate you asking me and the children to come with you, but we going to be just fine. My house be strong. It be standing through two hurricanes. And some of my neighbors who don't have men-folk around the house, they like to be coming to my place, if there's a storm. You just go along to the hotel, and take Mistress Mary with you. And you explain that I be coming to work as soon as the storm be over. She will understand. She always be nice with me."

I took her hand when the taxi stopped at the end of a sand road near her house. "Thank you for helping me tonight," I said. "I couldn't have done it without you."

"I'm surely glad I was with you, but I'm mighty glad it's over. Well, almost over. You get that thing to Mr. David just as quick as you can."

I said that I would. And I asked her again if she wouldn't like to get the children and come with me to the hotel until after the hurricane. But she said she'd be alright, and that she'd see me after the storm.

When we got to the beach house, I directed the taxi man to drive into the driveway and told him I'd be back in five minutes.

"I gotta get home, Mistress," he complained.

"I won't be long. The storm isn't going to come for a while yet. You'll have plenty of time to get home before it hits." I hoped I sounded more confident than I felt.

I felt the first stirring of the wind when I stepped out of the taxi. And so did he. He stuck his hand out of the window, sniffed the air, and said, "It be coming."

"Five minutes," I promised.

The house was quiet. Too quiet, because in the silence I could hear the palm trees rattling in the wind. I glanced at my watch: 2:45.

Samuel was curled up at one end of the big white sofa, asleep, his mouth partly open, his breathing deep and measured. I touched the top of his head. This was my brave protector. I'd let him sleep until Mary was ready. Then I'd wake him and bundle him off to the hotel with us.

It's almost over, I thought. I'll give the package to David. He'll give it to the police, and they'll arrest Whitey and Franklin . . . and Alan? He was a part of this, wasn't he? Well, then. I suddenly remembered that day on the beach when he carried me out of the water. I said, "You saved my life, Alan. How can I thank you?" "You can do the same for me some time." Was now the time? I'd talk to David. Surely he would understand that I felt a moral obligation to Alan. Perhaps he could do something, talk to someone.

And when all of this was finished, David and I would leave Jamaica. I would make no demands on him. I'd do everything I could to soften the edges of his grief for his son. I'd love him without demands.

When I knocked at Mary's bedroom door, she called, "Come in if it's you, Catherine."

"And if it's not?" I said as I opened the door.

"Then come in, whoever."

"My, you're brave! Come on—time to get up—we're going to the hotel."

"At this hour! Are you mad?" Her hair was blue-black and curly-crisp against the white pillow. Her skin shown from a recent scrubbing.

"You look nice," I said. Her nightgown was pale green and lacy. "You look like the illustration for a Cosmo article—'How to dress for your lover.' "

She smiled, pleased. "Where have you and David been? Did you know that Samuel is spending the night again?"

"David's been asleep for hours, I imagine. As for Samuel, we'll take him to the hotel with us."

She sat up. "What do you mean, 'David's been asleep for hours?' "

"I told him I was tired. He brought me back early." I sat on the edge of the bed. "I've been crime-busting, Mary."

"What in the world?"

"I told you Whitey and Franklin were up to something. Tonight I proved it. Another banana boat was being loaded. I went down to the dock. You should have seen your friend Franklin. No spic and span shoes tonight, kid. No jazzy white pants. Tonight he was just a 'po' ole', banana-totin' Jamaican.' " I paused and took a deep breath. "Bananas with a million bucks stuffed up inside them."

She hugged her knees and looked at me as though I'd gone crazy. "You're out of your mind," she said.

I reached into my case and pulled out the cellophane bag. "Here's part of it. The other part is still tied up at the docks. Thanks to Gladys."

"Catherine, you're the one who's bananas! Who in the world is Gladys."

"Gladys is a hurricane. That's why we're going to the hotel. And thanks to her, the ship won't be able to leave. By that time David will have notified the police and . . . But never mind that. I've got a taxi waiting. Hurry and put something on, while I wake Samuel."

"I'm not going anywhere, darling. I don't really believe the storm is going to turn into a hurricane. And I don't believe Whitey is involved in any of this business."

Rain lashed the window. "Mary, I saw him tonight. He was on his way to meet Franklin. Of course he's involved!"

"You don't *know* that, Catherine."

"Yes, I do," I insisted. "Now get dressed."

"I'm staying here. I think you're letting your imagination run away with you. First, you didn't like Alan. Then Whitey. Now you're suspicious of poor Franklin. Really, darling, I think the sun's been too much for you. Perhaps it's time you headed to New York."

She had an edge to her voice I'd never heard before. But I refused to get angry. "I'll leave just as soon as I can, Mary. I'm not going to argue with you now. But I am going to ask you to please come with me. We can talk about this later."

"We're not going to talk about it at all. You go run to David with your precious packet. What is it anyway? Coke?"

"Yes, I think so."

Outside, above the growing sound of the wind, a horn blew.

"That's the taxi," I said. "I've got to go."

"Then go, darling. I'm going to finish this book and go to sleep."

"Mary, please. That's a hurricane out there. It's going to get worse. Euphemia said the last one had a hundred and twenty-five mile an hour winds. Please come to the hotel with me. This house is too close to the water for comfort."

The horn blew again.

"I've got to get this package to David," I said frantically.

"Then run along." Her voice was cool.

"Please come with me."

Again she shook her head.

A great slash of rain hit the windows.

"Can't you wait until morning, Catherine?"

"No."

"Then, take my raincoat. It's in the closet. Right-hand side."

I put it on. I took the package of white powder and shoved it into the coat pocket. "I won't stay at the hotel," I said, "I'll have the taxi wait while I run up and get David. We'll both come back. I'll let Samuel sleep. You get up and put some clothes on. Make some coffee. We'll be back before the storm hits. O.K.?"

She smiled. "O.K."

"And we'll have a hurricane party. And tell ghost stories."

"All right, darling. We'll sit in the dark and tell ghost stories. Just the way we used to."

"Yes," I said. "Just the way we used to."

And then, I don't know why, I leaned over the bed impulsively and kissed her good-bye.

CHAPTER SIXTEEN

The front of the hotel was boarded up. The lobby was empty except for the desk clerk who sprawled, snoring, on one of the chairs. A light glowed from the lamp beside him. Next to it were candles and matches.

The two elevators were locked. I debated waking the clerk, but decided not to and headed for the stairs. Once again I had asked the taxi man to wait. This time he wasn't so patient.

"Pay me now, lady," he asked. "I don't have all night. I got to get home to my wife and children. They going to be scared white as vanilla wafers when this storm hit."

"Just a few more minutes," I begged. I handed him a five dollar bill. "I'll give you five more when I come back. Only, please wait."

I was out of breath when I reached David's door. I knocked, eager to see him, eager to see the expression on his face when I said, "Look what *I've* got."

I knocked again. And again. And finally I didn't knock, I *pounded*. And then I ran down the three flights of stairs. I shook the desk clerk and said, "I'm sorry. I've got to get into 305."

"Extra key behind the desk," he mumbled. "Help yourself." He began to snore again before I reached the desk.

I found the key, cursed the locked elevators, and made for the stairs again. "David?" I called when I finally unlocked the door. "David?" I reached along the wall until I found the light switch. "David?" I said again before I turned the light on. I didn't want to startle him. I thought that, even if he were in a deep sleep, the sound of my voice as the light went on would reassure him. But I needn't have worried. The room was empty.

I was so disappointed I could have howled. Here I stood with a package of cocaine or heroin in my pocket, while outside a hurricane was about to hit. I wanted David. I wanted him to get the police, stop the boat from sailing, and shelter *me* from the storm. To hell with Women's Lib. To hell with standing on my own feet. I wanted a man to take charge.

And what should I do now? Get back to the beach house, I supposed. Ride out the storm with Mary and Samuel and try to find David as soon as it was over. And if I couldn't find him, I'd go to the police myself. I'd leave a note so he'd know I'd been there. I had to find a piece of paper and a pencil.

The dresser and the top of the desk were bare. I opened the desk drawer and found a pencil but no paper. I looked in the wastebasket and said, damn, under my breath when I saw how clean it was. I went into the bathroom. Pieces of torn, yellow paper lay in the bottom of the wastebasket. In sheer desperation, I got down on my hands and knees, searching for a scrap big enough to write on. Suddenly two words hit me. 'White-haired . . .'

I dumped the pieces out on the floor, juggling them around, trying to fit torn piece to torn piece. I put as much of it together as I could and read:

> 'Proceed with . . . White-haired man
> your . . .'

And another torn piece with the word 'Sam.'

I sat back on my heels. So David *was* still an agent, just as I had suspected. Funny, I didn't mind as much as I thought I would. I should have known he wasn't the rye bread type.

'Sam,' I suppose meant 'Uncle Sam.' Somebody in the government had a peculiar sense of humor.

Now, more than ever, I had to tell him what I'd found. I picked out the biggest piece I could find and wrote: 'Important pkg. & info. Come to house.' And signed it 'C-with-a-C.'

I propped the note up on the dresser and hurried out and back down the three flights of stairs. I replaced David's key in it's slot behind the desk.

As I started past the snoring desk clerk, a gust of wind shook the hotel with terrible force. The lights flickered and weakened. I hesitated before the man's chair. Then I took a candle and a package of matches. In a low voice I said, "You don't mind if I borrow a candle, do you? Well, thank you. That's very nice of you, and I appreciate it. And a package of matches? Thank you ever so much. And a goodnight to you too."

The rain was harder now, slanting down in great sheets against the side of the hotel. I buttoned Mary's coat up around my neck and pulled the kerchief tighter under my chin.

The taxi was gone. There wasn't a car in sight. Just the rain, the bending palms, and the growing roar of the surf.

The road was a half mile from the hotel. The beach was maybe fifty yards. I took my shoes off and sped for the beach.

The palm trees bent away from the wind. I bent toward the wind. I carried my shoes for five minutes and then tossed them aside. I had all I could do to stay on my feet. The rain blinded me. I'd never known how dark dark could be. I prayed that the electricity would hold out until I reached the beach house. If it didn't, I'd never find it. I forgot everything else in my concern for that one most important thing in the world. Over and over I thought, please let the lights be on. Please let the lights be on.

A coconut thudded on the sand near my feet, spurring me to a gallop. Darn, darn, darn, if I hadn't told Mary I'd be back I could have stayed at the hotel. Pulled up a chair next to the happy snorer and waited for David to come back.

I was soaked to my skin and shivering with cold now. This was one hell of a night—or morning—to be out alone. Alone on a Jamaican beach in the middle of a hurricane. My teeth began to chatter. I concentrated every bit of my will power into unclenching my jaws.

Just as I was about to give up, I saw the flicker of light at the top of the sand dune. Mary's sand dune. I began to laugh with relief as I dug bare feet into the sand and climbed to the top.

The terrace was littered with palm fronds. A tree had fallen across one of the tables. Other porch furniture was overturned. "You're supposed to put things in the house during a hurricane," I heard myself say, as I stumbled across the debris and pushed open the door to the living room. Samuel sat huddled at one end of the sofa, a pillow clutched to his chest.

"Hi," I said. "Hi, Samuel."

Then I was on the floor beside him, weak with relief at seeing another human being. I got hold of myself and mustered a hearty, "Well. Well, well, well. This is some storm, isn't it?"

"Yes, ma'am, Mistress Catherine. And it going to be meaner any time now."

"It's going to get worse?"

"Yes ma'am. It's going to get worse before it gets better."

"Tell you what, I'll get Mary and we'll make some hot chocolate and peanut-butter-and-jelly sandwiches. How's that sound?"

His eyes still said he was frightened, but his voice said, "That will be just fine."

I took off the wet raincoat and kerchief and hung them over a chair. The matches were wet, but the candle was alright. I hunted for other matches. "I'm going to leave these here," I told Samuel. "If the lights go out, you light the candle. And could you look in the hall closet? I think I saw a flashlight in there the other day. I'll be right, back." I gave him another hug, more to reassure myself than him.

Mary wasn't in the kitchen. I wondered if she'd gone back to sleep. I didn't see how anybody in Jamaica could sleep through all the racket the storm was making.

A sudden gust of wind shook the house as I started down the hall. I remembered what Euphemia had told me about the people in Port Antonio who'd been washed out to sea in the last hurricane. The lights flickered.

"Mary?" My voice sounded puny. "Mary?"

No answer. Only the thundering whomp of the wind.

Her bedroom door was ajar. "Mary if you've gone back to sleep I'll . . ."

She wasn't in her bed.

I started around the side of it, my eyes intent on the candle beside the lamp, when my bare foot touched something wet. I looked down. I remember thinking what's wet and red and sticky? Like a riddle. A childhood riddle.

Blood, my brain answered. Blood is wet and red and sticky.

And Mary. Because blood is oozing out of her throat, down over her mint-green nightgown. Drip-dripping onto the floor.

Her face was bruised and swollen. Her dead eyes stared into mine.

"Don't," I said. "Please don't be dead."

I knelt beside her. I smoothed the crisp, black hair back from her bruised face. "Listen," I said. "I've got to go now. I've got to go because Samuel is waiting for me in the living room, and I don't want to leave him there alone because he's just a little boy and he's frightened, and I've got to go back to him and take him somewhere out of here, if we can still get up the beach, and I think I'll take him home and that's what I have to think about now, Mary, because if I think about you and what somebody has done to you and that maybe whoever did it is still in the house, I'm going to start screaming. Mary, Mary, Mary, I'll never for the rest of my life forget the way you look, but I've got to leave you now."

I put my hand over my mouth and squeezed hard to keep from screaming. Then I stood up and backed out of the room. And just as I did, the hall lights flickered again. And went out.

Darkness. Pitch black, cave-deep darkness.

And fear. A wanting-to-crouch-in-the-back-of-the-closet fear.

The house lurched in the wind, and thunder split the sky. But it wasn't the storm I was afraid of. It was Whitey. Whitey and a blood-stained knife waiting somewhere in this long corridor.

But I had to forget him now. And I had to forget Mary.

I felt my way, step by fearful step. At last I saw a flicker of light, and then the small face, the eyes white and round in the dimness of the living room. I squeezed his shoulder. When I asked him if he'd had any luck finding the flashlight, my voice was wobbly.

"I just be starting to look when the lights go out, and so I grabbed the candle."

"Good boy. You hold the candle and I'll look in the closet."

I found it on the top shelf, turned it on, and almost cried

with relief to see that its beam was good and strong. A windbreaker jacket hung in the closet. I put that on Samuel and zipped it up. "You know more about hurricanes than I do. Do you think we can go out in this?"

He chewed his bottom lip and finally nodded. "It be bad, but it going to be worse. I think if we go fast, we still got time. Where we be going?"

"To your mama's."

The relief in his eyes gave me the strength I needed.

I put Mary's wet raincoat back on. We were as ready as we'd ever be. Or were we? The wind sounded so strong, so wild, and Samuel was such a little boy. What if we were separated?

My eyes searched the room. I spotted the cords that held the drapes back. I pulled one off and told Samuel I was going to tie us together. I looped one end around his chest, under his arms, and tied the other end around my wrist. And then I said, "That ought to keep us together. Are you ready?"

He nodded. I knew he was frightened.

"I'm so glad you're here to help me," I said. "I don't know what I would do without you."

His voice was stronger when he answered. "We going to be all right, Mistress Catherine. I know the way in the dark. You just hang onto that cord and we going to be fine."

I blew the candle out and we stepped out into the storm. By the light of the flashlight we made our way down the sand dune to the beach. The first terrible blast of the wind knocked Samuel off his feet, and I thanked God I'd thought of tying us together.

Rain slashed at our bodies as we bent almost double into the wind. Lightning split the sky with jagged light, and thunder exploded against our eardrums.

We made our way close to the shoreline to avoid the coconuts that were falling all around us. When the lightning came, it showed an ocean I'd never seen before, rolling black waves, eleven or twelve feet high, lunging and pounding at the shore.

Samuel held tightly to my hand while the wind and the rain battered us. I'd been frightened before, but never like this. The wind blew Samuel off his feet. The rope tugged me down with him, and for a moment we were rolled like beach balls toward the sea. Finally, with his small body under mine, I dug my nails into the sand to stop us and, bent double, I managed to stagger to my feet and lift Samuel into my arms.

"How much farther?" I shouted into his ear.

His arms clutched around my neck, then loosened while he tried to peer through the rain. "Maybe not too far . . . bunch of trees . . . don't worry, Miss . . ." His words were lost in the wind.

Perhaps alone I couldn't have made it. I'm sure I couldn't have. I remembered Euphemia's words when I asked her if she wanted me to take Samuel to her. She'd said, "He be safe with you. I know you watch over Samuel like he be your own."

I felt his face against mine. Felt his thin arms as they clutched my neck. And somehow, somehow, I was able to summon every bit of strength and determination I had.

How long did I walk in that cruel night? How many times did I fall? How many times did I pick Samuel up and tell him everything was going to be all right?

I lost track of time. Samuel and I were trapped forever in a world of wind and sand, rain and darkness. But I would not stop. I would go on and on and . . .

Ahead of me I saw shadowy forms bending in the wind. I remembered Samuel's words, "bunch of trees."

Maybe these were the right trees, maybe they weren't. But I lurched toward them. Past them. No houses. Only slanting, blowing sand dunes. Struggling for breath, I screamed at Samuel to wrap his legs around my waist. I released my hold on him and clawed my way up the dunes. And there, just above the rise, were the houses.

"We made it," I shouted. "We made it, Samuel. We're going to be alright."

The wind was at our backs, propelling us toward the houses.

"Which one? Which one is yours?"

He lifted one hand from my neck and tried to see through the driving, rain. Then he pointed.

I made for the house. The wind helped us now. With one great gust it blew us against the door. I beat on it with my fists. "Euphemia," I called. "Euphemia."

The door was opened, and the two of us fell into her arms.

CHAPTER SEVENTEEN

I don't know how many hours we huddled together in the main room of that fragile house, Euphemia and her boys, the neighbors and their children. So many of us, each one drawing comfort from the others.

Euphemia took me into the bedroom and made me take my wet clothes off and dry myself. And she gave me a clean calico dress and a pair of sandals. I wanted to tell her about Mary, but she had so many people to look after, so much comforting to do, that I could not bring myself to add to her worries. 'After the storm,' I thought, 'after the storm I'll tell her.'

And so I sat with the other women while the storm beat down around us, Samuel close beside me. Moses, who was frightened enough to be almost friendly, picked Bruce up, and the two of them came and crawled onto my lap.

At mid-morning the wind lessened, then stopped.

"It's over," I said.

Euphemia shook her head. "No, Mistress. This be the 'eye.' A hurricane be shaped like a donut. One part of it come, then there's the hole in the donut, and pretty soon the other part come. Most times it be harder than the first part. If you like, we can step outside a bit and look around."

"Would I have time to get to town? It's important."

"Go to town? Lord, no, you must stay close to shelter so

162

when the wind come again you be safe."

"But it's important. Look, I have to talk to you alone. When I explain, you'll see why I have to go."

We went outside and I told her about Mary. "She was there on the floor beside the bed," I said. "Her face was bruised and cut. She didn't even look like Mary." I had to wait a moment or two to steady myself. "And he'd slashed her throat." I was crying now, crying so hard I could barely get the words out. "Why? Why? Why? She *liked* him, she actually liked him."

"Lord God," she said. "Lord God, Mistress Catherine." She bowed her head and said, "Sweet Lord Jesus, take Mistress Mary to your bosom, rock her in your arms, and tote her off to heaven in a big white carriage."

And then she folded me into her arms and let me cry until all the tears were gone. When I stepped away from her, I wiped my eyes with my fist and said, "She's all alone. I can't leave her there like that. I've got to go to the police. They've got to catch that white-haired duppie bastard." I tried to choke back a new flood of tears.

"As soon as the storm be over, you and me together, we find the police and we go take care of Mistress Mary. But for now you going to bide here with us."

After the noise of the hurricane, the quiet was almost eerie. The damage in this small community was devastating. All that remained of Euphemia's white picket fence were two, lone upright sticks. The ruby red bougainvillaea that climbed from ground to roof was torn from the house and lay in bleeding shreds. Houses that belonged to two of the women I'd met at Euphemia's were gone. They'd simply disappeared. One woman stood in the middle of what had once been her front yard, staring at the empty space in front of her, a low keening emanating from her throat. While Euphemia tried to comfort her, I went to the edge of the sand dune and gazed down at the rolling, monstrous waves.

So much had happened in such a short space of time. I saw again in my mind's eye the way Mary looked when I found her last night. I tried to cast out that vision of her and replace it with the way she had looked when I'd first returned to the house—clean from the shower, vivacious and lovely. But that other, awful picture forced it's way back into my mind. I made myself examine it. There were bruises on her face. Had she struggled? Why had he beaten her? I knew who "he" was. I knew who had killed her. There had been no question in my mind that it was Whitey. Whitey, whose stock in trade was a knife.

When had he come? Why had he come? If only I had insisted she come with me to the hotel. If only I'd dragged her from her bed and said, "You're coming with me whether you want to or not." If only.

But I'd come to find David. David! I'd almost forgotten him in the shock of finding Mary's body and the terror of the storm. Where had he been? Where was he now?

A hand slipped into mine. I looked down to see Samuel.

"Mama say we better go in. The wind going to be coming for true."

The wind came for true. Stronger and harder than before. As the day wore on, the straight wooden chair cut into my back. In spite of the terrible noise of the wind and the trembling of the house, I found myself nodding. Euphemia asked me if I wanted to go to the bedroom, but I said no, I'd rather stay in the crowded front room. She fixed me a pallet on the floor. I lay down and was about to drift off, when Moses curled up beside me. Euphemia started to drag him away, but I said, "No, he's fine." I put my arm around his waist and went to sleep.

I woke to blessed silence, the tickle of a curly head under my chin and a fluff of orange tail across my arm. The wind had stopped. The neighbors had gone. Moses and Bruce and I were alone. I closed my eyes, then opened them when Euphemia came into the room. "He be here," she said, "and everything going to be all right now."

David, I thought. Oh, thank God.

I almost cried with disappointment when Alan stepped through the door. He ran across the room, and before I could move, he was down on his knees beside me, gripping my arms and pulling me to a sitting position. Moses let out one loud indignant roar and struck out at Alan. Startled, Alan who laughed and said, "Your mama's gone back out in the yard. You go find her."

Moses gave him a baleful look, wiped his nose with the length of a small hand, picked up the hissing cat, and marched out the door.

Alan gave me a little shake. "Are you alright?"

"Yes." I tried to comb my fingers through my tangled hair. "How'd you know where to find me? Samuel and I made it just before the worst of the storm hit. What about you?"

His left hand was bandaged, and his face was scratched. "Are you alright? You look terrible."

"I'm O.K. I was half way between here and Kingston when the storm hit. I thought I could make it, but just the other side of Port Maria the wind blew the car off the road. I landed in a ditch." He shook his head. "I've never seen anything like it, Cathy. The wind took everything that wasn't nailed down. Palm trees bent to the ground. Coconuts flew through the air like bullets. I just flattened out and held on until the first part of the storm was over. This morning I hitched a ride to Ocho Rios." His eyes avoided mine. "I went to the house first. When you . . . When I didn't find you there, I thought of

Euphemia. I figured you'd be here or she would know where you were."

"Then you . . . you've seen Mary?"

He bit his lip. "You saw her that way? You found her?" He reached for me. "God, Cathy, God, I'm sorry."

"I shouldn't have left her alone, but Samuel was waiting in the living room and the storm was getting bad. The lights went out and I was afraid he . . . he might still be there in the house with that damned bloody knife . . . and I didn't know what to do, so I took Samuel and ran. I shouldn't have. I should have gone for help. I should have . . ."

"Cathy, don't." He pressed my face against his shoulder so that I couldn't speak. I felt his lips against my hair.

When I moved away, he said, "Are you alright? Can you tell me about it? What time did you find her?"

I took a deep breath to steady myself. "I returned to the house the first time at 2:45. I'd been to the docks and I wanted to go to the hotel to find David. I stopped at the house to try to get Mary to come with me."

"Wait a minute. You said you were at the docks? But you weren't with David?"

"No, I went alone."

"Alone! Why?"

"Well, not really alone. Euphemia was there and . . ." I found myself wanting to pour everything out, to tell him all that had happened. I'd almost forgotten that he was part of it. That he worked with Whitey and Franklin. In a way, he was as much responsible for Mary's death as Whitey was. I drew away from him.

"Cathy, answer me. What were you doing at the docks?"

"I'm sorry, Alan. I can't tell you."

"Look, Cathy, if this has anything to do with Mary's death, you'd better tell me."

"You're the last one I'd tell," I said bitterly.

"You really don't trust me, do you? You don't even like me." He stood up. When he spoke again his voice was brisk. "Well, I can't do anything about that. But I need your help. You're holding something back and I've got to know what it is."

He reached into his back pocket and pulled out his wallet. "I'm a narcotics agent, Cathy. Whitey thinks I'm a buyer for an Eastern syndicate. That's why I've had to work with him."

He handed me a card.

United States of America. Treasury Department. A photograph. And under the photograph the name, Alan M. Carlisle.

I stared at the card, unable to believe what I saw. Angry because he hadn't told me. "You should have told me," I said.

"I couldn't. I'm sorry. Now, please, tell me what you know."

And so I told him about going to the dock and about the white powder I'd found. "I think its cocaine," I said.

Mary's raincoat was on a hook near the door. I pulled the package out and handed it to him. "This was stuffed up the stem of the hand of bananas. There must be thousands just like it. I don't know how many trucks Franklin unloaded before I got there. As soon as I left the warehouse I went to David's hotel to try to give it to him, but he wasn't there. I wanted him to get the police and stop the ship . . ." I swallowed. "I hope he's alright. So much has happened . . . Well, is that what it is? Is it cocaine?"

He hefted the bag in his hand. Then he opened it. "It's cocaine, all right. Cocaine, the new status drug for some eight million people. Ten per cent of all high school students snort it. Ten bucks a snort, Cathy, and the effects only last thirty minutes. A real snorter will use it every thirty or forty minutes.

"We knew it had to be transported out of here by ship, but before we made a move we wanted to get the whole organization, from the growers to the shippers—*and* the receivers. Now, thanks to you, we know how it's loaded. Franklin puts it in a specially designated section of the ship; somebody on the other end knows exactly which section."

"Where is this shipment headed? Do you know?"

"Miami, probably. It's the cocaine import capital of the country. People smuggle coke in inside hairdryers, fishing rods, aerosol cans, books, tennis rackets, even diving tanks."

"But it's so risky. Why would anybody take the chance?"

"Money. A ten thousand dollar investment in ninety-seven per cent pure cocaine can make a man three hundred and twenty thousand dollars."

"That much? The ship is still here. It wouldn't have been able to leave because of the hurricane. You can still stop it."

He shook his head. "No, we'll let it go. I'll alert agents at the other end, and we'll nab that part of the operation too." He looked triumphant. "And that ties it up, because I've found the source here. Franklin knows the Cockpit Country like the back of his hand—that's where the stuff is grown."

"I know. I've been doing research for a book. I wonder what it's like up there?"

"Wild. Beautiful. Like you're on another planet." He hesitated. "That's where I've been, Cathy. I lied to you. I took Laura and Kitty and Mark to Kingston. Then I went up into the Cockpit Country. I know where the stuff is grown and how it's shipped out—down into Kingston. I know the laboratory where it's processed. And you've found out how it's shipped out of Jamaica. That about wraps it up."

"Whitey? How is he involved?"

"He's the head man here in Jamaica. A million-dollar shipment came in the night you walked in on us. I didn't know what he might do. I couldn't believe it when you walked into the kitchen. That's why I . . . said what I did."

"But now you've got him. You've got them all."

"Whitey, Franklin, all the men in between." He reached out and took my hands. "I have to tell you something, Cathy. You've got to know that . . . David . . . Cathy, David's involved too."

"David!"

"We've known it for a long time."

"What in the hell are you talking about?"

"They're a team, Cathy. David and Whitey. We've been on to them for over a year."

I stared at him, unable to speak. "David's an agent," I said finally.

"He used to be."

"He still is!" I was shouting now. "I saw a cablegram. It said . . ."

"I don't know what it said, but it wasn't from the government."

I looked into his green eyes. I felt my fingers curl into claws. "Whitey killed Mary, and now you're saying that he and David work together. That David would . . . How can you say such a thing? How can you . . . ?" My voice was a low hiss of anger.

He put his hands on my shoulders. I jerked away from him.

"We'll talk about it later," he said, "when this is over. I'm going to the police now. I only stopped, here to try to find you. I'll come back as soon as I can. Meantime, I want you to wait here."

"I'm going back to the house," I said.

"If you don't promise me right now that you'll stay here, I'll take you in to the police and have you held in protective custody until this is wrapped up."

I glared at him. Hating him.

"Is that clear?"

"Quite clear."

"Will you wait here?" His voice was hard.

I looked him square in the eye. "I don't have any choice, do I?"

"None. I'll be back as soon as I can. It may not be until tonight or tomorrow. I'll explain to Euphemia why I want you to stay here."

"No, I'll tell her. She won't mind."

"I know. She's a very special kind of person. Cathy, about David . . . we'll talk about it when I come back. Maybe there's something I can do."

I turned my back. I didn't see him leave.

I waited ten minutes. I told Euphemia that Alan had the package of cocaine and that he was taking care of everything, but that I was supposed to meet him back at the beach house. When she tried to protest to say that she would come with me, I told her no, that Alan wanted me to come alone. I held her hand and thanked her for her kindness. I gave the protesting Moses a kiss and told him to take care of Bruce. I kissed Samuel too and told him that no, positively, he could not come with me.

I didn't know why Alan thought David was mixed up in this terrible business, but it had to be straightened out. I had to get to David to tell him about Alan's accusations. If the phone at the beach house was still out, I'd go to the hotel.

The sea splashed angry, gray waves high onto the deserted beach. I found myself retreating farther and farther from the shore. Dusk came early, and the sky was suffused with flamingo pink rays as the sun settled over the horizon.

In spite of myself, I stiffened when I saw the house standing silent and bleak over the rise of the dune. I shuddered at the thought of entering. I would not go to Mary's room. I would enter by the French doors of my bedroom, try to phone David, change clothes, and leave the way I'd come.

Over-turned tables, smashed chairs, palm fronds, coconuts, seaweed, and broken glass littered the terrace. The windows at the front of the house were broken, one side had been smashed almost flat by a giant tree, and most of the red tile had been ripped off the roof. Alexander Montgomery's gift to Mary. As twisted and broken as she was.

I made my way along the terrace, stepping over debris. The French doors were open, the floor wet where rain had blown in, the curtain splattered and torn. This was the room that I had loved, where I had been loved. I hated to look at it now.

I knew that the phones were probably out, but the silence when I picked up the receiver was still a shattering disappointment.

I'd have given my teeth for a shower, but I wanted to get to David before Alan did, so I stepped out of Euphemia's blue calico dress and ran to the bathroom to splash water on my face and run a comb through my tangled hair.

Outside dusk settled into darkness. I flipped the light switch. Nothing happened. Now I hurried, not wanting to spend one minute of darkness in that house. I pulled a pair of pants, a blouse and a pair of sneakers out of the closet. I was buttoning the blouse when I heard the steps on the terrace.

I froze. I looked for a place to hide. Closet, bathroom, shower, under bed. For one fleeting second I tried to tell myself I was foolish.

Then I remembered the pinched malevolence of Whitey's

face. And Mary's bruised and ruined body.

The steps came closer.

I stepped into the closet and pulled the sliding doors too.

I heard the French doors being pulled wide. Steps in the bedroom. Retreating to the bathroom. Returning. Then silence, as though whoever it was was trying to decide what to do next. The steps moved to the wall.

I stayed where I was, wondering why he hadn't heard my heart racketing in my chest. Cautiously I slid the doors open. As tempted as I was to run, a part of me wanted to see who it was. Step by careful step I moved to the hallway.

The door to Mary's room was open.

I peered cautiously into the almost-dark room. A man was bending over the sheet-shrouded body.

I know I should have turned, should have run for my life, but I was frozen.

Then, as in slow motion, the man turned toward me. And stretched out a hand.

The sound of a moan. Was it me? Yes, the sound came from my throat. And the sound became a word. And the word was "David."

CHAPTER EIGHTEEN

We couldn't speak. We just hung onto each other for a long time. Finally he led me out of the bedroom into the living room, where we sat close together on the long white sofa. When I lifted my head from his shoulder I said, "Are you alright then?"

"Yes, but I've been half out of my mind worrying about you. I found your note." His arm tightened around me. "You know about Mary?"

"I found her last night. This morning I mean. After I came back from trying to find you."

"I'm sorry, Catherine. So sorry. I tried to get to you last night. I had to go out after I took you home. By the time I realized how bad the weather was going to be, I got stuck. If I'd known about Mary, I'd have come in spite of the storm."

"I know, darling."

"What time did you come to the hotel?"

"I'm not sure. I know I came back here the first time at 2:45 and . . ."

"Wait a minute! I brought you home at eleven. I figured you came to the hotel later because of the storm. Do you mean you went out after our date?"

"Yes, but . . ." I sat up and pulled away from him. "So did you. And when I got to your hotel at three-or-so you weren't there."

"That's different."

"If that isn't just like a man!"

"Come on, Catherine, why did you go out again? Where were you?"

"I went down to the docks. I was suspicious of Franklin. I told you I'd seen him the night we went to watch the banana loading, but you wouldn't believe me. I told Euphemia to tell me the next time a ship was in. I'm sorry I didn't tell you, darling, but I knew if I did you wouldn't have wanted me to go."

"You're goddamn right I wouldn't have!"

"That's why I didn't tell you. I went alone, and I watched Franklin. He loaded bananas from just one truck. When he went down toward the ship, I talked to the driver while Euphemia swiped a hand of bananas. We looked through them and found a package of white powder stuffed up into the stem and . . ."

"Where is the package now, Catherine?" His voice was cold, low, and calm.

"I gave it to Alan."

He slammed his fist down on the coffee table. "Why in the name of God did you do that?"

"I tried to find you, David. That's why I went to the hotel. I wanted to give it to you so that you could go to the police. But you weren't there. I came back here and found . . . Mary . . . found Mary dead. And the storm was getting worse and worse. I was afraid Whitey might still be in the house. I just took Samuel and ran." I swallowed. "Then, after the storm, Alan found me at Euphemia's and I gave the package to him."

I covered his hand with mine. "But it's alright. He's a narcotics agent. He showed me his credentials and . . ."

His hands gripped mine with terrible urgency. "When did you see him? How long ago?"

"An hour maybe. We argued. He told me to stay with Euphemia while he went to the police." I tried to choke back my rising panic. "He's got a crazy idea about you, and I wanted to find you to tell you so . . ."

"What kind of an idea?"

I loosened his grip on my hands and faced him. "He thinks you're working with Whitey. I told him how wrong he was, but he wouldn't listen. We'll see him together. We'll . . ."

How can any words explain the change that came over him? The tightened jaw, the narrowed eyes, the vein that throbbed at his temple?

"Don't be upset, darling," I said, aware that my voice was shaking. "When you tell him . . ." But he wasn't listening to me. I felt my chest constricting. Each breath I took was painful.

"Where were you last night?" I asked.

"I had to go out. I had to see somebody."

"Whitey?"

He didn't answer. He didn't meet my eyes.

"I saw him at the dock. He was there, and then he was here. He killed Mary, didn't he?"

"Yes. Probably."

I tried to swallow my pain. "Why?"

"I don't know. When did you see her last?"

"At 2:45. Here. She was in bed. I wanted her to go with me to your hotel, but she wouldn't. I was gone—forty-five minutes, perhaps. The storm had already started when I left your hotel. I found her when I got back."

"Did you tell her about the cocaine?"

"Yes, I showed it to her. I tried to tell her about Whitey, but she wouldn't listen. My God, David, she was sleeping with him. She *liked* him. Why would he kill her?"

"Maybe because he couldn't get his hands on you."

I stared at him in horror.

"We're getting out of here. I've got a car outside. We can

rent a boat in Port Royal and make it to Cuba."

"Cuba! We don't want to go to Cuba!"

"Just for a few days, Catherine. I've got friends there. We'll be alright."

"But I don't want to go to Cuba." What was happening? I felt suddenly off-balance, disoriented. I didn't understand what was happening. The panic that I'd felt earlier gripped me. "Look, David," I said, "let's wait until Alan and the police come and . . ."

He grabbed my wrist and pulled me to my feet. "We're leaving, Catherine. Now. You're going to do exactly what I tell you to do. Whitey is still in Ocho Rios. I want you out of here."

"But the police . . ."

"Damn the police! Now go on into the bedroom and throw a few things into a suitcase. Just what you'll need for a few days. We'll get what we need later."

"But why? David, tell me why."

"I haven't got the time to explain." He avoided my eyes. "You'll just have to trust me."

"Yes, I guess I will," I said slowly.

I didn't understand what was happening. I didn't know why David wanted us to leave without waiting for the police. I'd seen the cablegram. I knew he was an agent.

Why didn't Alan know David was still an agent? Were there two branches of the government working on the same thing? And one didn't know about the other?

My head was a jumble of so many thoughts—all of them on a collision course. And why Cuba?

It's odd, now that I think about it, that while I questioned David's motives, it did not occur to me to tell him that I would not go with him.

I took the flashlight he had given me, moved down the hall

to the bedroom, and began putting things into a suitcase. Two pants suits, a couple of blouses, a skirt, a sweater. I couldn't think. My sketch book. The sketches I'd made of Samuel.

I sat on the bed and put my head in my hands. I wanted to tell Samuel goodbye. And Euphemia. Oh Lord, how I wanted to see Euphemia.

And the sketches I'd done for my book on Jamaica? I'd never finish them now.

But at least I could make sure that the sketches of Samuel got to the publisher. They were for Mary's last book, and I was going to make sure the book was published. I tore a page out of the pad and scribbled a note to Alan:

> Will you see that these get to Mary's publisher? I have to go away. With David. You're wrong about him, you know. He would never work with a man like Whitey. I wish I could explain. Perhaps some day we'll get together over a long cool Planters' Punch and I'll be able to.

So many things I wanted to say. Instead I added, "Thank you, Alan." And signed my name. Cathy instead of Catherine.

Makeup. Shower cap. A pair of shoes.

I glanced quickly around the room. The clown David had given me sat on top of the dresser. He looked at me with his sad, droopy eyes. I touched his red ball of a nose and whispered. "I guess we're going to Cuba." I put him in the suitcase.

It wouldn't close. I took the shoes out.

"Catherine!" David's voice was urgent.

"I'm coming." Frantically I glanced around the room. I grabbed my purse off the chair and crammed drawing pencils into it.

"Catherine!"

The door to Mary's room was closed. I hesitated in front of it, but I didn't go in. There would be time to think of her later, I told myself. Now I had to think of David.

He'd made sandwiches. "For the trip," he said. "Things are probably still closed down in Port Royal. I've fixed a thermos of coffee too. You ready?"

I swallowed hard. "I guess so."

He lighted some candles and placed them on the mantle over the fireplace. They flickered against the mirror on the wall above it, giving the room a look of eerie unreality. David was looking away from me, out toward the sea. He had such a solid, *big* look about him. I wondered why I felt so alone. So utterly desolate. I needed assurance now, as I had never needed it before.

I said, "David . . ."

He turned around and looked at me for a long moment. "Trust me," he said. "Just trust me."

And this is what loving is, I thought.

He picked up my suitcase and started toward the fireplace to snuff out the candles, when I heard the sound. I raised my hand in a wait motion.

"What is it?"

"I don't know," I whispered. "Something. It sounded as thought it came from my bedroom."

"Maybe the wind blew the doors open."

"The doors were already open. There isn't any wind tonight." My throat went dry. "Somebody could have . . ."

"You're imagining things."

"No."

Behind him the candles flickered. I looked towards them, and there, in the mirror, I saw him. Saw the evil face. The flat, gray eyes. The lips parted in a Mephistophelian smile.

I couldn't move. I couldn't turn to see if the face in the

mirror was the reflection of the man or of my fear. I could only stare at the face above the wavering candles.

"I see you found her," he said.

"She found me," David said.

"Franklin told me she was hanging around the loading shed last night." His eyes swung to me. "You find anything interesting while you were there, Catsy?"

"I went to make some sketches. That's all I did."

"You didn't poke your pretty nose in where you shouldn't have? You didn't try to con anybody? A truck driver, maybe?"

I could scarcely breathe. "I don't know what you're talking about."

His eyes bored into mine. I made myself meet his look as calmly as I could.

"You're a lying little bitch," he said, "but I haven't got time to find out what you're lying about." He turned to David. "As soon as Franklin told me about seeing her, I beat it over here."

"And found Mary," I said.

He nodded. Smiling. "The black kid is asleep on the couch, so she takes me to her bedroom. She's looking very delectable, just a thin robe over her nightgown. So I push her back on the bed and . . ."

I put my hand out in front of me, trying to stop his words. "Please," I said, "please don't tell me . . ."

"I push her back on the bed," he said deliberately, "and I give her a one, two, three bang."

"Knock it off," David said.

"Shut up!" He didn't even look at David.

"When she gets her breath, she wants to know am I smuggling coke. And I say, 'Smuggling? Who's smuggling? I'm in the shipping business. I ship coke. I ship hash. I ship H.'

"She smiles a little and she says, 'So Catherine was right about you.'

"Then I tell her I got a little something to discuss with you, and I ask her where you are. She stops smiling. She tells me to get the hell out of her house. I say I'll be glad to go just as soon as she tells me where you are. She shakes her head and she says, 'No way, you son of a bitch.'

"I slap her around. She won't say anything. I hurt her real bad. I squeeze nerves she never knew she had. I even make a few cuts on that doll face of hers so she'll know I mean business. She's crying and hurting and swearing and sweating. But she won't tell me. And I know that no matter what I do to her, she isn't going to tell me where you are."

He yawned deliberately. "I stuck a knife in her throat."

"Whitey, for Christ's sake . . ." David said.

He had spoken calmly. So unemotionally. 'Pass me the butter. Pour me a beer. I stuck a knife in her throat.'

I was aware that tears were streaming down my face. I was aware of David's face, so white, so still, so anguished. Then all awareness stopped. The room tilted as I slumped to a chair. I took deep gasping breaths and willed myself not to faint. David was beside me, holding me. His face was close to mine. "You've got him now," I said.

Whitey's laugh cut through the room. "Who's got who?"

The silence in the room was broken only by the gentle brush of palm fronds against the window.

I looked at David. Why didn't he say it? Why didn't he say, 'You're all through, Whitey. You're under arrest?'

But he said nothing.

"I saw the cablegram," I was desperate now. "I saw the cablegram from the government."

Whitey sniggered. "I gotta tell Sam you took him for a government cop." He moved across the room until he stood almost directly in front of me. "He's our Miami contact, lady. He sent the cablegram."

His grin was wolfish. "*Our* contact," he repeated. "Mine and David's.

In the terrible stillness of the room a candle hissed and went out.

"You're lying," I said.

"Am I? Tell her, Dave. Tell her I'm lying."

"Catherine . . ."

"Tell her!"

He didn't have to. I saw it in his face. But I heard him say, "I'm not a cop, Catherine. I haven't been for a long time. I work for a drug syndicate out of Miami."

"Oh David," I whispered. "Oh David, why?"

"I had to. He knows where Davey is."

I stared at him. Not understanding. "How can he know!" I said at last. "You said Davey was missing in action. Nobody knows where some of those men are. What could possibly . . . ?"

"He used to smuggle opium out of Laos. He knows the area. The right people. He swears he can get Davey out." His eyes met mine. "I'll do anything I have to to get Davey back. Anything."

He took a deep breath. When he spoke again his voice was strong. "Now you know. And you know why you have to come with me. You won't have to be involved in what I do. I'm sorry about Mary—sorrier than I can ever tell you. But I'll make it up to you. In time you'll forget."

"I'll never forget," I said.

"Yes, you will. It's going to be all right. We'll be together. My cut of this is going to be two hundred thousand dollars. I'll take you anywhere you want to go. I'll buy you anything you want."

I closed my eyes, trying to blot out his face. "I loved you," I said.

"Jee-zus!" Whitey sneered. "You're breaking my heart."

"She's going to come with us," David told him. "She won't say anything. She'll do whatever I tell her to do."

"No, I won't," I said. "Not now."

"You satisfied, Dave?"

"I'm taking her out of here," David said.

"Is that right?" The voice was deadly.

"We'll meet you in Cuba." He picked up my suitcase. "Come on," he said, without looking at me.

"I'm not going with you," I said.

He took hold of my arm and propelled me toward the door.

"Stop right there!" Whitey said.

"Get out of my way," David said. "Get out of my way, you freaky son-of-a-bitch."

"Dave!" He chuckled, "You don't want to talk to me like that, pal. You. want to see your kid again, don't you?"

David let go of my arm. "Go to Euphemia's," he said. "Wait for me there."

"I'll go. But I won't wait for you. Not now. Not ever." I turned my back on him and started toward the door.

"You take one more step toward the door, Catsy-baby, and I'm gonna blow your goddamn head off."

I saw the gun in his hand. I didn't move.

"Put it away," David said.

"You want to see your kid again?" Whitey's words were clear and cold.

David's face looked frozen.

"I ask you, you want to see your kid again?"

"Yes." He swallowed painfully. "I want to see my kid again."

"Then you follow orders. A plane's coming to St. Ann's Bay at four-thirty tomorrow morning. It'll fly us to Cuba. We stay there a couple of weeks, and then we ease into Miami."

"I won't go without Catherine."

"O.K., O.K., you want to take the broad along, that's your business, if—and here I gotta stress the if—*if* you keep her under control. If you don't, we waste her."

"No . . ." David's face was ashen.

Whitey moved closer to me, so close that when he spoke I could smell the dry foulness of his breath. "That would be a shame," he said softly. "We got some gorgeous girl-type stuff here." He ran his hands up and down my arms. "You know what I want to do to you, don't you Catsy?"

"Whitey, so help me God, if you don't take your hands off her . . ."

He laughed. "I'm clowning, Dave. You know I'm not serious. I told you, she's yours as long as she behaves herself. Now, let's haul ass out of here before the cops show up."

"I'm not . . ." I started to say. But of course I was. I had no choice. Just as David had no choice. The two of us were caught in a trap as old as time. David was trapped because he loved his son. I was trapped because I loved David. And Whitey knew it. He knew he had us exactly where he wanted us.

CHAPTER NINETEEN

Normally St. Ann's Bay is an hour's drive from Ocho Rios. But that night, after the storm, the narrow highway was almost impassable. Debris of every description lay across the road. Where there wasn't space for the car to pass, Whitey drove off the road, sometimes easing off the soft side, skirting the sand that had drifted onto the pitted pavement, other times slanting the car wheels at an almost impossible angle on the mountain side.

Since I could not detach myself physically, I tried to detach myself emotionally. David held my hand, but I did not respond to the pressure of his fingers. It was as though something inside me had dried and frozen. I was alone on the narrow space of seat, fleeting through the darkness to . . . I didn't know. I didn't care.

And this man who sat beside me? This man who held my hand in his. I had loved him. I had held him gently in the night, as he had held me. Now it was finished. I would not go with him to Cuba. I would not go anywhere with him. Because, in a strange way, if I accepted what he was now, then this is what he would be for the rest of his life. And the part of the man who could hold a woman with gentleness, or touch a child with love, would surely die.

I would weep for the man he might have been, but I would never accept the man he was.

More than two hours passed before we turned off the highway onto a narrow dirt road.

"Where are we?" David asked.

"Used to be an estate," Whitey told him. "Some English muckety-muck. Lord Jamison-Ettles. House was built about 1820. Back when they had slaves and could operate a joint like this. When the slaves were freed, most of these places went busted. Musta been a hell of a joint in it's day."

It was still a hell of a joint, I thought. A big white mansion surrounded by moss-draped trees, thick bushes, and weed-choked lawns. A forgotten Tara. Long porch, tall white columns, wide-shuttered windows. Standing alone, quiet and forgotten in the still night.

"End of the line," Whitey said. "This is where we stay till the plane comes." He took a flashlight out of his pocket and led the way around to the back of the house. Once he turned and flashed the light in my face. "You get a good grip on her, Dave. We don't want to lose her."

"She won't run away," David said. His hand moved to clasp my wrist.

Whitey took a key from his pocket and opened the back door. "Follow me," he ordered.

We moved through a black hall. Suddenly I knew where we were. This must be the gambling club that Mary had told us about, closed now because of the storm. Strange that they used only the cellar, and for a gambling house. Why hadn't somebody thought to renovate and make it into a hotel? There must have been dozens of rooms.

And all of them dark, I thought suddenly.

If I could break away from David, surely I could find a place to hide. The plane was due at four-thirty. Light wouldn't come till five-thirty or so. Whitey *had* to get on that plane. If I could hide till then, I'd be safe.

But I had to make my break soon. If he led us down to

where the gambling rooms were, there'd be some kind of light—oil lamps or candles. It was now or never.

I took a deep, steadying breath, turned swiftly, and raked my nails across the hand that held my wrist. David gave an involuntary cry and released me. I ran past him, back the way we came, running blindly in the dark, my arms out in front of me.

"Son of a bitch!" I heard Whitey cry. "I told you . . ." I ran into something, a table I think. But it caught me hip-high and I didn't fall. I felt my way around it, darting a glance back as I did to see the spot of light that meant Whitey was moving toward me.

I ran as fast as I dared into the blackness in front of me. My foot caught something, a footstool perhaps, and I stumbled and fell, twisting my wrist, banging my knee. I struggled to my feet, feeling blindly around me. I'd never known darkness like this. I felt as though I were blindfolded, in a maze, with deliberate obstacles set in the path before me, so that no matter what I did I could not escape.

"Catherine!" I hesitated at the sound of David's voice. "Catherine!" I swear I won't let him hurt you. Stop running. Tell me where you are. I promise you, Catherine . . ."

I ran into a wall. No, not a wall, a door. I could feel that it was a door. The smack of my hands seemed to reverberate through the house. I searched for the doorknob. Up and down, waist high. Higher. Lower. God. Oh, God. Sobbing in frustration, ready to turn away when my hand found the knob. I pulled hard, opened the door, and ran headlong into a wall. I had run into a closet.

"Klutz," I silently screamed to myself as I slumped to the floor, sick with disappointment and fear, my heart pounding so violently I could hardly get my breath.

I heard the steps. Heard David say, "We'll find her."

"You're goddamn right we'll find her. Now shut up and listen."

Now the sound of their feet. A thud. A whispered, "Damn!" as one of them ran into something. A beam of light. Moving closer. Stopping. Swinging to the right, hesitating, and then back. "Hey, that door. Maybe she . . ."

And then the light moved into the closet, around and down, down into my face.

Whitey reached in and yanked me to my feet. "You little bitch," he snarled. "I haven't got time for your goddamned games." He slapped my face, once, twice, three times before David stopped him. He shouldered David away and thrust me ahead of him, his hand tight and hurting on my arm, back down the hall, down the stairs to the cellar, pushing me the last few steps so that I fell.

"Get the lamps," he told David, swinging the flashlight to a side cupboard. And to me, "You move an inch and I kick you senseless."

I didn't move. In the light of the lamp I could see the gaming tables and slot machines. Chandeliers hung from the ceiling. Chairs, high-backed and cushioned, spotted around the room. The carpet was soft and plush beneath my hands.

David came to me. He bent down and pulled me to my feet. He smoothed the hair back from my face.

"That did it, you know," Whitey said. "I'm not going to take a chance on her."

"Look," David said, his voice tight with tension, "she'll be O.K. once we're out of here. I'll do whatever you want. I'll drug her. I'll tie her. We'll put her on the plane, and she won't know a thing until we're in Cuba."

"What are you going to do then? How long you think you can keep her doped up? How long you gonna keep her tied?

The minute you turn your back, she's gone running to the cops."

"She'll be all right, I tell you."

"You tell me nothin'! You got into this thing because you want your son back. And if you still want him back, you do what I say. And I say she's dangerous and she's not going to leave this cellar till the club opens up again and somebody finds her. By then she'll be too busy playing her harp to talk."

His eyes raked mine. "I'm kinda sorry, Catsy. I had a real yen for you. You know?" He moved closer. "If there was time, I'd take you over in the corner where your boyfriend couldn't see us. If you were real nice to me, I might even decide to let you live." One hand reached out and cupped my breast.

I struck out and caught him on the side of the face with the back of my hand. I've never wanted to kill anybody before, but oh god, I wanted to kill him. "You bastard," I spat. "You murderer. You filth. I'd die before I let you touch me."

A muscle twitched in his jaw. "You may have to," he said.

And to David he said, "Kill her."

I heard David's indrawn breath.

"You want your son back, Dave? You want him home again?" He watched my face as he said the words: "Then you kill her."

David looked at me with desperate eyes.

"Don't you see what he's doing to you?" I said. "It's been five years. How do you know Davey's even alive?"

"Don't say that! He *is* alive. Whitey told me. He promised me he'd get him back."

"There's the only way I'm going to do it now, pal." The voice was a hiss. "You want your son, you kill her."

David reached into his coat and pulled out a small snubnosed gun.

"Thatta boy," Whitey said. A small gathering of spittle ran

from the corner of his mouth. "I had a letter from Cambodia yesterday. For a hundred grand and the name I give you, you got Davey home free."

David's face was white and still. He raised the gun.

Thoughts skittered inside my head.

He's going to kill me. David is going to kill me. I'm going to die.

Terror. Hate. Disgust. Anger. Pity. Sorrow. Love.

Will it hurt?

Please . . .

A sudden knowing.

And I wanted to tell him. Tell him that Whitey was lying, that he could never get Davey back. But I knew, even now, in my horror, how deep his love and his grief were. He would believe what he wanted to believe. And he believed Whitey could perform the miracle that would restore his son to him. I knew that in his mind he had no choice, and the part of me that sorrowed for the man he might have been wanted to say, kill me gently, darling. Kill me gently.

Our eyes held.

Then, as if in slow motion, he swung around and pulled the trigger.

I saw the white eyebrows raise in surprise, saw the white face twist in anger, saw the red stain explode in the middle of the narrow chest, saw the knees sag, saw the white arm raise. Saw the spatulate finger squeeze.

And I heard the whomp sound as David's own body slammed against the wall.

I knelt down. I cradled his head in my arms. I told him again and again that everything would be alright.

He looked up at me through death-misted eyes. "Remember . . . remember the clown . . ."

I kissed him. I took the breath from his lips.

And later, sometime, I don't know when, I went out to the car and drove back to Ocho Rios. To Euphemia's.

Alan found me there. After I told him all that had happened, I said, "He told David there was a letter from a man in Laos. He said he'd give David the letter if David would . . ." I couldn't go on. "Would you find out, Alan? Would you find out if there is a letter?"

"There's no letter, Cathy. Whitey didn't know anybody in Laos. He never had any idea where Davey was."

But I knew. I knew where Davey was. I knew that David had found his son.

I went alone to Port Antonio and Mandeville to do the sketches I wanted to do. Then Euphemia and I rode the train to Look Behind and made our way into Cockpit Country.

Finally, when it was time to leave, we held each other's hands, and I knew that something beautiful comes from everything that happens to us.

I didn't look back when the plane circled low over the turquoise sea. I didn't want to see my Island in the Sun fade from my sight. I thought of New York, of what I would do now. Without Mary. Without David.

When the plane landed at Kennedy, I moved along with the crowd toward the terminal. When I heard my name, when a voice said, "Cathy . . ." I turned and saw that it was Alan.

"How did you know I was coming?"

"Euphemia called me."

"I might have known," I said. But when I saw his look of uncertainty, saw that the mocking grin had given way to a serious, almost awkward look, I said, "Do you suppose there's a place in New York that makes a decent Planter's Punch?"

"We'll see," he said. "We have plenty of time to find out, haven't we?"

"Yes," I said. "We have plenty of time."